The Convenient Mail Order Bride

Chance at Love Series, Volume 1

Ruth Ann Nordin

Published by Ruth Ann Nordin, 2023.

Dedication: Joanie Watson Dixon who has a very kind heart. It's always a joy to talk to you.

Chapter One

March 1878
Cincinnati, Ohio

Phoebe Durbin turned the page of the mail-order bride ads in the catalogue. She wasn't sure what she expected when she purchased it from the merchant of the general store, but she didn't have any other option.

Money. I should be concentrating on the men who have money.

Or at least a property and good home they actually owned. She shifted on the bench outside the store, ignoring the slight sting of conscience that told her money wasn't everything.

No, it's not, but you can't eat good intentions. You can only eat food, and the only way to do that is to have money to purchase it.

She wasn't afraid of work. A woman's labor in the house was never done. Men came home from the factory and enjoyed the rest of the evening in comfort. Mothers and wives fussed around them and gave them whatever they wanted. And as long as the man wasn't gambling or carousing with women, Phoebe saw no harm in it.

Most of the advertisements were brief—so much so that she couldn't get a good idea of what the man was like. Granted, there was limited space for them to write, but she had hoped there might be something—anything—that would tell her who would be the right man to marry.

"Any luck yet?" a woman asked, approaching the bench.

Phoebe shook her head. "Not yet, Ma. What did Phillip say?"

Her mother sat beside her. "He can't afford a bigger place. I'm afraid we can't stay with him once the baby is born."

Phoebe did her best to hide her disappointment. Her brother did well at the factory, but with a wife, two children and one due in two months, his apartment was cramped as it was. She and her mother couldn't keep living with them. It was enough he'd let them stay with them for the past year.

She had to find a husband, and since there weren't any suitors vying for her hand, she had to pick one out of a catalogue full of ads.

"How does this sound, Ma?" She cleared her throat and summarized the ad. "This one is from a widower who has three children who need a mother. He owns a hundred and fifty acres and has a nice cabin by a stream."

"He sounds like a nice man, but it'll be easier if you don't marry someone who already has children. Your aunt married a man with two children, and they never did come around to thinking of her as their mother. Up to her death, they resented her for taking their mother's place even though their mother passed away when they were young."

That was true. She didn't want to end up like Aunt Eunice who'd died last year. Sadly, neither child would attend the funeral to pay their respects.

"You're right," Phoebe said. "I'm going to ignore all the ads with men who have children."

"I'm sure some of those men and children would be nice, but you just can't tell who they are from an ad, and we don't have time to waste on a lot of letters to sort them all out."

Phoebe smiled. "I already agreed with you, Ma. You don't need to keep trying to convince me."

Her mother chuckled and squeezed her hand. "I thought I should explain myself better."

"You explained yourself fine the first time. Now, let's see who else is looking for a wife." She scanned through the ads until one caught her eye. "This one doesn't sound so bad. Here's a man who owns his own land, has a cabin, animals, and his own well. He is also a good hunter. He's twenty-three and has never been married. He's looking to settle down with an honest, good woman he can start a family with. His name is Abe Thomas." She lowered the catalogue. "What do you think, Ma?"

"He sounds better than any of the others you told me about."

"He does, doesn't he? Why don't I send him a letter and see what he writes back?"

Her mother nodded. "I think that's a good idea. But before you do that, read through the rest of the ads and see if there's anyone else who sounds as promising."

Phoebe didn't think there would be, not by a long shot, but she turned her attention back to the ads and continued scanning through them.

THREE WEEKS HAD PASSED when Phillip came through the door with a missive in his hand. Phoebe, who'd been telling her three-year-old niece and six-year-old nephew a story, looked up from where she was sitting on the couch as he held it out to her.

"I got a missive already?" Phoebe asked, not believing her eyes when she saw the envelope stamped all the way from the Colorado Territory.

"The man you sent the ad to must've been happy to read your letter," her brother said. "He knows a good woman when he comes across one."

She smiled at her brother's compliment and took the letter. She stared at the handwriting on the envelope. The man wrote clearly. She had no trouble reading her name. Her thumb ran across his name in the upper corner. Abe Thomas. What was he like? She wondered if he sent a picture. She'd had one made and included it in her letter to him. She thought it only fair he know what she looked like, and she'd asked him to send a picture in return so she'd know what he looked like as well. Perhaps he'd thought it a strange request, but she hoped he'd obliged her all the same.

Beatrice came in from the kitchen, rubbing her pregnant belly. "What is it?" she asked, approaching them.

"Abe sent me a missive," Phoebe told her. Then, with an uneasy chuckle, she added, "I'm afraid to open it."

"He wouldn't have written if he wasn't interested," Beatrice teased.

"Open it, Auntie," her nephew, Ben, insisted. "Open it!"

"Oh, um, I will." Phoebe glanced at the letter again. "But maybe I'll do it after dinner."

"Nonsense, do it now," her brother encouraged. "You can read it in my bedroom if you'd like some privacy."

After a moment, she nodded. "Alright." She'd never be able to focus on dinner if she didn't. Wondering what was in the missive was likely to drive her to distraction. "I will. Thank you."

She went to her brother and sister-in-law's bedroom and shut the door. On the other side, she could hear Ben asking what was in the letter and Beatrice laughing as she told him he was too young to worry about it.

Phoebe closed her eyes and waited until her heart wasn't hammering quite so fiercely in her chest to open them. It was just a missive, and as Beatrice said, Abe wouldn't have sent a reply if he wasn't interested.

Gathering courage from the thought, she went over to the small rocker by the bed and sat down. She'd taken the time to respond to two more ads after she'd answered Abe's, but his had been the first. As silly as it was, it made his reply that much more important.

She turned the envelope over and opened it, careful not to tear it lest she rip the letter or, if he'd sent it, a picture. When she was done, she pulled the neatly folded paper out and inside was a picture, as she'd hoped. Excited, she turned it over in her hand and inspected it.

He had dark hair and a nice face, but it wasn't at all what she'd expected. He looked awfully young. He was probably fourteen when it was taken. Frowning, she turned it over and nearly fainted with relief. In script was the date the photograph was taken, and it'd been taken nine years ago, which put him at twenty-three now.

Good. He'd sounded so nice in the advertisement. Really, he'd sounded much more promising than the others she'd replied to, so she was hoping he'd be the one. But before she could get her hopes up, she needed to read the missive and see what he'd written.

Right away she could see he had nice handwriting. That in itself was a promising sign. So far, so good. She held her breath and read through the letter.

Salutations, Miss Durbin,

I found your response to my ad most promising. I have no trouble taking on the responsibility of caring for your mother. There's plenty of room in my cabin. One thing I considered when building it was starting a family some day. I always knew the bachelor life wasn't for me, even back then. My mother, God bless her soul, instilled the value of a good lady. One who honors her own mother, the way you do, is just the kind I'm looking for.

Besides that, I will admit you're quite lovely to look at. Your picture is very pleasing to the eye.

Heat rose up in her face from the unexpected compliment. She'd never thought of what it might be like to have a man tell her she was pretty, but now she knew it was immensely satisfying. Smiling, she continued reading the missive.

I wish I had a more recent picture of myself to send you, but alas, I don't. I do hope, however, seeing even the younger version of me will give you an idea of what you'll be getting into should you choose to marry me.

I'm a hardworking, honest man of reasonable means. I might not have struck it rich with the gold out here in the Colorado territory, but I can provide you and your mother a comfortable living for the rest of your life. The cabin is mine, and the ten acres is mine as well. There is a nice stream on the land where you can get water, bathe, and do laundry. From time to time, I'll catch fish. Mostly I hunt and grow my own food, and I'm adept at cooking.

I forgot to mention I have a well. In fact, I just dug up a new one a year ago, so you don't have to go back and forth to the stream each time you want water. I might not have all the conveniences you probably enjoy back East, but I do live comfortably. You won't have to ever want for anything.

I hope you and your mother will consider coming out here. In case you do, I've included two tickets for you both. From the train station, you will have to take a stagecoach but I added money for that. If you decide you'd rather marry another, there's no need to repay me.

Looking forward to your reply,

Abe Thomas

Phoebe checked the envelope, and sure enough, two tickets and money were there, and the tickets were set for three weeks from now. That would certainly be enough time for her and her mother to get their things in order and pack. It would also solve their problem on what to do when Phillip's baby was born.

She lowered the missive and considered what her life might be like with him. He sounded like a good, decent man from what he'd written. But was he the best choice? Maybe he'd received other replies to his ad. No, that was nonsense. He wouldn't have sent her the tickets if he had. Or maybe he had received other replies but picked her.

At any rate, it wouldn't make a difference. The choice was now hers and her mother's. She stood up just as someone knocked on the door.

"Come in," she called out.

The door creaked open and her mother's head poked into the room. "I heard you got a reply from one of the men you sent a letter to."

"Yes." Phoebe waved her in. "It's the one in the Colorado Territory."

Her mother came into the room and shut the door behind her. "What do you think?"

"I think he might be the one. He sounds really nice, and he said he's more than happy to provide for both of us." She held the letter out to her. "Read it and tell me what you think."

"It doesn't matter what I think. What matters is what you think. You're the one who has to marry him and have his children."

"I know, but I'd like to hear your thoughts."

"Alright." Her mother chuckled and took the missive.

As her mother sat down, Phoebe asked, "You're back from the doctor's early. Does that mean he gave you a good report?"

"Yes, it does. He said I got a strong constitution, which is good if we're going to be living far out West."

"It is."

And it was good since most of the ads came from men out West. Phoebe had worried the trip and poor living conditions out there wouldn't be good for her mother and had insisted on the doctor's visit, just to be sure.

Phoebe went over to the small window in the room and looked at the brick street where children were playing. Women were lingering nearby, talking to their friends, and the apartments were close together. In her brief reading about the West, she knew there was much land out there.

People lived far apart from each other, unless they were in town, and even then, towns were small. It was nothing like she was used to. There were conveniences she'd have to give up, like being able to walk to any store she needed or going to social engagements with her friends. But her friends weren't any better off than Phillip. They were all struggling to make ends meet. It just hadn't been the same since her pa died.

She would marry one of the men who posted those ads because she had to. If she could find love in the process, it'd be all the better. And she thought she could love a man like the one who'd sent that missive. As for the Colorado Territory, she didn't know if she'd like it or not, but she knew she could adjust to it. She could adjust to anything, really, if she was surrounded by people she loved.

"He seems like a nice young man," her mother said, breaking her out of her thoughts.

Phoebe turned back to her and smiled. "He does, doesn't he?" She released her breath. She hadn't even written to him to let him know she was coming, and her heartbeat was already picking up in apprehension. She wasn't sure what she should tell him. "Should we wait and see if any more replies come back?"

"The tickets aren't until three weeks from now. If we haven't received a better reply, we'll take that as a sign we're to go to the Colorado Territory."

She nodded. It sounded like a good plan. She saw no reason not to do it. She only hoped if they did go there, Abe was as good as he sounded on paper.

Chapter Two

Three weeks later

"I can't believe you're leaving," Phillip told Phoebe at the train station platform. "Are you sure you're alright? You look flushed."

"I'm a jumble of nerves," Phoebe admitted, putting her hand over her stomach where it seemed as if the butterflies would never stop fluttering wildly. "I can hardly concentrate."

Her mother put her arm around her shoulders and gave her a reassuring squeeze. "It's a big risk, there's no denying that."

"If it doesn't work out, you can always come back," Phillip told them.

While Phoebe appreciated the sentiment, she knew it wouldn't be possible. There was no way he could keep taking care of her and their mother. He was barely managing as it was. He was a good brother, always doing whatever he could, but she and her mother had both decided they wouldn't come back, no matter what happened. They'd find another way to make a life out there. That being the case, it also meant she would never see him, his wife, or her dear nephew and niece ever again.

Swallowing the lump in her throat, she gave all of them a hug. She couldn't bring herself to say good-bye, though they all knew it was happening. Saying it would only make her cry, and she didn't want to do that until she was on the train.

"I'll send a missive when I get there," she said after she cleared her throat.

"We both will," her mother added.

"You're very brave to do this," Beatrice told Phoebe. "I don't know if I'd have as much courage."

Phoebe clasped her hands. "I'm sure you could if you had to, but," glancing at Phillip, she smiled, "you'll never have to. You two are steadfast and true."

"I hope your marriage will be a good one," Beatrice replied, her voice soft.

Phoebe hoped so, too, but she was too afraid to say it aloud. She took a deep breath and released it. "Let me know the baby's name and birthday. Ma and I will send the little one something special."

"I will."

Phoebe hugged her niece and nephew again, this time telling them to be good and obey their parents.

The conductor announced it was time to board the train. Forcing down the nervous flutter of butterflies in her stomach, Phoebe made another promise to write to them then led her mother to the train.

Abe had been thoughtful in giving them good seats in the passenger car. They would have a comfortable ride out West, and while a part of her couldn't deny the sense of adventure that waited for her, another part was terrified she was making the biggest mistake of her life. This was a huge moment. She was about to meet the man she'd marry. This would be the man she'd have children and grow old with. He'd be a big part of her life. And to think she hadn't even met him yet.

"You'll be fine," her mother assured her, placing her hand over hers. "Deep down, I can feel it."

Phoebe forced herself to smile. She hoped her mother was right. There was nothing more she wanted than to look back on this moment a year from now and be grateful she took such a risk. And maybe she would. Maybe this would be the best thing that ever happened to her.

UPON HER ARRIVAL AT the small town in the Colorado Territory, Phoebe had the sinking sensation her decision to come out West was the worst one she'd ever made.

"What do you mean Abe Thomas isn't expecting me?" she asked Carl Richie, who'd met them at the stagecoach.

At least Carl had the decency to look contrite as he said, "I wrote the ad and the letter on his behalf."

Of all the scenarios that had played out in her mind during her trip, not a single one prepared her for this.

Phoebe glanced at her mother, whose eyes were wide in horror, then turned her gaze to the few buildings and dirt road that made up the town stuck in the middle of a bunch of trees. Only a couple of people loitered on the boardwalk where the stagecoach had dropped her, her mother, and their trunks off. That stagecoach was still there, but neither she nor her mother had the money to buy a ride back to the train to take them back home.

Phoebe turned her gaze back to the man. "Since that's the case, you'll be paying for us to go back to Ohio."

If she wasn't in such a state of shock, she might be suitably upset with him. But as it was, the shock was holding her in place, preventing her from acting in a very unladylike manner.

"I sort of used all my money to get you out here," Carl explained with what he probably thought was an adorable shrug.

She, however, found nothing adorable about it.

"But he needs a wife," Carl quickly said, as if this made up for everything. "He's been by himself on ten acres and a large cabin. He has more than enough room for you and your ma."

"He might have enough room for us, but what if he doesn't want us?" Phoebe snapped, finally getting angry enough to let him know she wasn't at all happy about this. He might have thought it was a good idea to lie, but she didn't. And she seriously doubted Abe Thomas would either when he found out. "You never even bothered to ask if he wanted you to place the ad for him," she added.

"Oh, he'll want you when he sees you," he replied, scanning her up and down with more interest than he had a right to. "You're prettier than any other lady around for miles. Why, if I weren't married, I'd consider hauling you off to my home right now."

Once more, a spark of anger shot right through her, and this time she didn't snap at him. This time, she smacked him on the head with her drawstring purse.

"Ow!" His hand went up to his head just before his hat fell off. "What'd you do that for?" He picked his hat up. "I was paying you a compliment."

"Some compliment," her mother said, giving him a good whack with her own purse. "You were undressing her with your eyes. You have no business doing that since you're not Abe Thomas."

"It's as Ma said. No business at all," Phoebe replied, thankful she had her mother here with her. At least they could put their heads together and come up with a plan on what to do next. "I believe we have better things to do with our time than talk to this crow." And that was exactly what he looked like with those beady little eyes and the large nose and wiry dark hair. "I'm glad you're not Abe Thomas," she told him. "Someone as pretty as me can't be mismatched with someone like you."

A round of chuckles caught her attention. She spun around in time to see a tall, imposing man heading her way. She narrowed her eyes at him when she noticed the doors to the nearby saloon doors swinging. He wasn't drunk, so she guessed he owned the place. After all, the owner made money off of getting men drunk, not from drinking.

Well, he'd better not think she'd be willing to offer her services in a soiled place like that. She'd heard horror stories of women who had to offer their bodies for a piece of bread out West. Such a thing would never happen to her. Even if she had to scrub outhouses, she'd never be a prostitute.

"You might as well get out of here, Carl," the man said. "You've caused enough trouble already."

"You of all people know Abe Thomas needs a wife," Carl told him. "It'll be good for him to mind his own affairs."

"That's not for you to decide. Run along. I'll clean up the mess you made."

Shoulders slumped, Carl gave her one last pathetically apologetic look then scurried off like the rat he was.

She would have enjoyed the defeated expression on his face had the situation not been so grim. She looked at her mother, wondering if she trusted this new man who was going to supposedly help them. Her mother gave a slight shake of her head, and Phoebe sighed in disappointment. So her mother wasn't sure if they could trust this stranger any more than they could've trusted Carl.

"I'm a lady," Phoebe told him, deciding it was just as well they get this over with as soon as possible in case he planned to haul her off to the saloon. "I came here to be a wife, not a prostitute."

Taking off his hat, the man said, "I didn't mistake you for a prostitute."

Sensing the sincerity in his tone, she relaxed. "Alright." She took a deep breath then said, "Do you know Abe Thomas?"

"It's a small town," he said. "Everyone knows everyone around here. I'm Eric Johnson. I'm the sheriff."

"Sheriff? But I thought you owned the…" Her voice drifted off in embarrassment as she considered another reason why he might be in the saloon. Perhaps he'd been with a prostitute, though it surprised her he'd do such a thing while it was still daylight. Didn't men like him usually wait until it was dark? She cleared her throat. "Well, it doesn't matter. What's important is what to do about Abe Thomas. Do you think he'll want a wife?"

"It'd be hard to say no to someone as pretty as you."

She frowned, not sure how to respond to that.

"I can see you don't know if you can trust me or not," he said. "I was in the saloon because I needed to talk to the owner. There was a brawl last night. Believe me, you don't want to know the details."

"We thank you for not giving them," her mother replied.

He grinned. "You two got spirit. I think you'd do well with Abe Thomas. He doesn't care much for weak women...I mean, ladies. I'll take you on out to his place, but I want to talk to him before he meets you. It'll give me a chance to soften him up."

Soften him up? Phoebe didn't like the sound of that, but what choice did she or her mother have? They had to at least try. If Abe said no, they would figure out what to do then.

"I'll come back with a wagon to load your trunks," he said, "then we'll head on out. He's a good thirty minutes away, so you'll want to take care of any personal needs now."

As he turned to leave, her mother spoke up. "You'll be bringing along a preacher, won't you? In case he says it's alright, I want to make sure my daughter's reputation is protected."

"Ma'am, this isn't like the East," he said. "We're far removed from civilization out there. No one cares about reputations."

"I care." Then after a moment, her mother added, "Don't you got a preacher in this town?"

"A traveling one, and he won't be due out here until two or three weeks. If you're concerned about your daughter's reputation, make sure you stay in the same room with her. Believe me. No man wants to touch a lady who's sharing a room with her ma."

Phoebe didn't like this new turn of events. She turned to her mother as he went across the street. "Maybe we should stay at an inn until the preacher gets here. I have a little money left over."

They searched through the small town, and to their despair the only place that also served as an inn was the saloon. Phoebe didn't know if she could bring herself to spend a single night in a place where men would be getting drunk and finding a room with a prostitute. Just the thought made her sick to her stomach.

Eyes filling with tears, she asked her mother, "What did we get ourselves into?"

"Now, now, you can't blame yourself," her mother replied, putting her arm around her shoulders. "Neither one of us knew Carl was deceiving us. If it'd really been Abe who posted the ad and wrote the missive, we'd be just fine."

Shaking her head, Phoebe dug out a handkerchief from her purse and dabbed her eyes. "This is terrible. We can't even get on a train. We'd have to wait for the stagecoach to come get us, and the driver said he won't return for a month."

"We'll do as Eric Johnson said and make sure to spend the night in the same room at Abe Thomas' house."

"If Abe Thomas is even willing to let us stay there."

At this point, she didn't know if their luck would even get them that far. Things were quickly going from bad to worse, and she was afraid of how much worse things were going to get before the day was done.

"We'll think of something," her mother promised. "It's a thirty minute ride out to Abe Thomas' place. That will give us time to think."

Her mother was right. Everything was happening so fast. They needed to take a moment to calm down and consider all of their options. But first, they had to find out what Abe was like and see if he'd be willing to marry her. They mustn't get ahead of themselves. One thing at a time. She took a deep breath and released it. They just had to take it one thing at a time.

Chapter Three

Abe Thomas pushed back his long black hair over his shoulder. Had he known he was going to end up fixing a hole in the roof when he came into the barn, he would have pulled his hair back.

He struck the hammer into a good part of the barn roof and groaned. Why was he letting his morning run-in with Carl Richie ruin his day? All he'd needed was a few items from the general store, and Carl started telling him other items he should buy.

"You should get more staple items like flour, sugar, and coffee," Carl had said as he followed him.

"If I want your opinion on what to buy, I'll ask," he'd told Carl. "Or better yet, you give me the land and stream that's rightfully mine."

Carl, in turn, had denied Abe had any rights to them and left.

Abe shook his head and sat back on the roof, his gaze going down to the section of land at the bottom of the gentle slope that bordered the row of trees. The trees were young, having been newly planted. But they included that stream and land, and those belonged to him. Carl put those trees there as a sign, but nothing could change the truth.

The sound of a horse's neigh took Abe's attention from the row of trees to a wagon coming onto his property. He narrowed his eyes. Between the trees, it was hard to tell who it was. All he knew was that there were three people in that wagon.

To be on the safe side, he climbed down the ladder and grabbed his rifle. Then he checked to make sure it was loaded. Going to the small window, he slid the end of the gun through the lower left corner, careful not to be obvious. He held his breath and focused through the sights.

The wagon was winding its way along the path leading to the barn. That was good. He'd get the intruders exactly where he wanted them.

His finger caressed the trigger of his gun. If it was Gene Carter, he'd pull the trigger without hesitation. Gene was worse than Carl, and that was saying something considering both weren't worth a pound of dirt.

After what seemed like some very long few minutes, he finally saw the driver of the wagon. Eric Johnson. He relaxed and lowered the gun. He put the gun back on the rack and headed out of the barn. As soon as he realized Eric had two women with him, his steps slowed. What was Eric doing bringing them all the way out here?

Though the question was on the tip of his tongue, he patiently waited for Eric to pull the wagon to a stop a few feet from him. Eric instructed the women to wait in the wagon, set the brake, and then jumped down.

"How are you doing, Abe?" Eric greeted.

"I don't know. What are they doing here?"

Eric glanced at the two women who quietly sat close together, one considerably older than the other. The bonnets on their heads blew in the breeze, and Abe detected a few blonde strands that had come loose from the younger one's bun. The older one whispered to the younger woman who nodded and squeezed the older one's hand. It was a tender gesture, one his mother used to give him. They must be mother and daughter.

"Can we talk in the barn?" Eric asked, his gaze going to the open doorway.

"Alright." Abe led the way into the barn, choosing to stand in the area that allowed him to see out the window without the women seeing him. "What's this about? You never brought any women out here before."

"I don't know how to best explain the situation, so I'm just going to come out and say it. Carl posted a mail-order bride ad on your behalf."

It took a moment for Eric's meaning to sink in. Eyes wide, he gestured in the direction of the wagon. "Are you telling me that young woman out there thinks she's going to be my wife?"

"Well, not really."

"What do you mean, 'not really'?"

"She believed she was going to marry you, but she thought you posted the ad and wrote her a missive telling her to come out here. Look," Eric took his hat off and wiped the sweat from his brow, "I wouldn't have brought her out here under other circumstances, but as it turns out, she and her mother don't have anywhere else to go. They were both deceived in making the trip to this territory. I didn't promise her you'd marry her, and she knows you might say no. But I thought it wouldn't hurt to talk to you."

Abe shook his head and glanced out the window. The young lady's head was bowed toward her mother's, and the two were quietly talking, probably lamenting the possibility their fate was in the hands of a half-breed. They were as white as white women could get. There was definitely no mix of Indian blood anywhere in their lineage.

"Why don't you marry her?" Abe asked, finally turning his gaze back to Eric. "You're white. Her life will be easier if she marries you."

"I already posted a mail-order bride ad."

"That's an even better reason for you to marry her."

"It would be except I already started a nice correspondence with one. She's as down on her luck as that woman out there is." He put the hat back on his head. "I got a chance to talk to the woman on my way out here, and I think she'd make you a good wife. Her name is Phoebe Durbin, and she came from Ohio. Her brother can no longer support her and her mother because he has a wife, two children, and one on the way. Phoebe had no suitors back there, so she answered a few ads. Whatever Carl wrote about you, it must have been good because she said you sounded like the most sincere and nicest man from the missives she received."

Abe couldn't help but laugh at the irony. Sincere and nice? How did Carl manage such a feat? "Did she bring the missive he wrote?" he asked.

"She did, but I didn't read it. I didn't feel it was my place to get that personal."

"Alright. Stay here." Abe left the barn and went straight to the wagon.

The two women stopped talking and watched him as he approached them. He had to admit the young one was pretty. Maybe even beautiful despite the fact that she was so pale. But that was to be expected since she likely wore hats and bonnets to protect her face from the sun, as he'd seen other white women do.

His interest at the moment, however, was in the missive Carl wrote, so he wasted no time in asking about it. "Eric said you got a missive that was supposedly from me?"

"Yes," she softly replied then pulled the strings of her purse open.

He noticed her hands trembling and wondered if she was afraid of him because he had some Cheyenne blood in him or if she was afraid he'd tell her and her mother to get off his land.

She finally dug the neatly folded paper out of the purse and handed it to him. "I-I didn't know Mr. Richie wrote it."

He snorted. "I wouldn't exactly call him 'mister'. He doesn't deserve the respect."

He took it from her and turned back to the barn. He wasn't willing to tell her he didn't know how to read. Yes, he knew a few words, but the script was more like scribbles to him. Once in the barn, he handed it to Eric.

"I want to know exactly what the sincere and nice Carl wrote," Abe said. "Don't leave anything out."

"I won't," Eric replied. As he opened it, a picture fell out. He stooped down to get it.

Curious, Abe leaned forward and saw an old picture of him. He frowned. Where did Carl get that from? He thought his mother had been the only person who had a picture of him. Unless she'd given one to his father. He gritted his teeth.

Eric began reading the missive, so Abe forced his attention to what he was saying. His eyes rose heavenward as he listened to Carl's lies about Abe's planning for a family when he built his cabin. His uncle had built the cabin for his mother. She'd always wanted a big one, so he'd added the extra rooms for her sake, though he'd often thought it was a waste of space.

"There is a nice stream on the land where you can get water, bathe, and do laundry," Eric read.

Abe stopped him. "That's another lie. Sure that stream is rightfully mine, but he won't let me have it. The poor woman has no idea she'd have to do all her bathing and washing from the well water."

"He does mention a well in the next paragraph. Want me to read it?"

"Yes." He might as well hear the whole thing. Then he'd know exactly what she'd been promised.

When Eric was done reading the rest of the missive, Abe turned his attention back to the woman and her mother.

"I'm going to talk to her," he told Eric as he took the paper full of half-truths. He nodded for the man to follow him, and Eric obeyed. Once he reached the wagon, he directed his gaze to Phoebe. "Can I talk to you over there?"

He gestured to the spot outside the barn. He didn't think she'd talk to him alone inside the barn so he figured if he gave her an open area where her mother could keep an eye on her, she'd be more likely to leave the wagon.

She offered him a nod and extended her hand toward him so he could help her down. Good grief. The woman was wearing gloves. She was as prim and proper as they came. She was in for a rude awakening to what life would be like if she stayed here. Things like gloves and fancy dresses just weren't practical. Biting back the comment, he took her hand and guided her down.

He led to her to a spot where they wouldn't be overheard and handed her the missive. "It seems Carl left some things out," he began, setting his hands on his hips.

"He left out a lot, like him not being who he claimed to be," she replied. "I really believed you wrote this."

"I know. It's in Carl's nature to lie. He's just like his pa." He sighed. "I don't know what to do. So I'll give you some options, and you tell me which one you want, alright?"

She slipped the missive back into the purse then clasped her hands together. "Alright. What do you propose?"

"One thing I could do is help you and your ma return to Ohio. Carl was right about me not having much money. I don't value gold like the white men do."

"White men? Aren't you white?"

"No. My pa was. My mother was Cheyenne." He paused. "Can't you tell I have Indian blood in me?"

"Your skin is darker, but I thought you had a lot of sun on you, like some of the other men I've seen who don't always wear a hat. You aren't wearing a hat right now."

"I don't like hats. My ancestors didn't wear white men's hats. But the fact that I'm not wearing a hat shows you my hair is darker than white men's."

"I've seen men with black hair before, though I admit they always cut it short."

"Where you come from, are there any Indians?"

"I've never ventured outside the main area of Cincinnati." She shrugged and cleared her throat. "My knowledge about these things is limited."

"You haven't heard anything about the savage Indians out West?" She blinked at the bitter tone that found its way into his voice, so he forced it back down. "I'm not saying Indians are savage. They aren't. All we do is try to protect ourselves as you white people keep taking land that belongs to us. And when we protect our land, you call us savage."

She didn't seem to know how to respond to that, and her look of surprise told him she hadn't been told much of anything about what was going on outside the small world she'd grown up in. She'd been sheltered from the truth her entire life. It would be wrong to direct his anger at her.

"Forgive me. I thought all white people were told the same thing about us," he said, his voice quieting down. "Would you like to return to Ohio? I don't have much money, but I do have enough to provide a way back for you and your mother. You might be more comfortable with your own people."

He fully expected her to take that option, so he waited for her to accept his offer. But instead, she asked, "What else can I choose?" When his eyebrows furrowed, she explained, "You said we have a couple of options. I'd like to hear what else there is to choose from."

Having caught him off guard, it took him a few seconds before he could reply. "Oh, well, I suppose we could get married, but you don't know what you're asking in doing that. You'd be marrying a half-breed. Out here, that's not a good thing. Eric's one of the very few who'll talk to me. The others try to pretend I'm not there, if they aren't talking down to me like I'm too dumb to understand them. On top of that, I'm a bastard."

"A bastard?"

"It means my parents weren't married."

"I know what it means. I just can't recall anyone saying the word so casually before. It took me by surprise when you blurted it out so matter-of-factly."

"Then that's something you ought to consider about me," he told her. "I tell it like it is. I learned long ago if I'm going to keep what's mine, I need to blurt things out, whether people want to hear them or not. I don't know what kind of place you grew up in, but around here, if you aren't ready to fight for what you have, you're going to lose it. I'm not sure that's the best option for a gentle woman and her mother."

She lowered her gaze and stared at her hands for a long moment. When she finally spoke, the tears in her voice made him wince. "My mother and I can't return to Ohio. We don't have the money to support ourselves, and my brother is doing all he can. I can't impose on him and his wife anymore." She brushed away a tear. "What other options do I have?"

With a sigh, he said, "You can stay here and answer another mail-order bride ad, and hopefully, this time it'll be from the person he claims to be. There's no one else around here I'd recommend you marry. Eric is already promised to a woman back East, and Travis is too scared of women to take a wife. I'm sorry to say this, but you're too pretty to stay in a home with one of the families in town. None of the wives would want to give you a room. Besides that, your only other option is to get a job, but you don't want the kind of job a single woman around here can get."

"I know. I've seen the town." She sniffed and dabbed her eyes again. "You don't want to marry me?"

His jaw dropped. She was really considering that option? If he was her, he would have searched more mail-order bride ads. Setting his arms at his sides, he said, "I'm a half-breed and a bastard. Life with me won't be an easy one. I never would post a mail-order bride ad. The last thing I want to do is curse someone with my life."

She glanced around his land, her gaze pausing when it passed over her mother who was talking to Eric. Her mother happened to look her way, and there was a private message that seemed to be exchanged between them.

When she turned her attention back to him, she said, "You take care of your cabin and barn."

Not sure where she was going with this, he ventured, "Yes. They're my cabin and barn."

"So it would be safe to assume you take care of your things?"

"If I don't, they'll fall apart."

"And when we were coming up here, you were on the roof. Were you fixing it?"

"Yes. There was a small hole up there. I noticed it after last night's rain."

"The horse looks well-fed."

He glanced at the steed in the fenced property behind the barn. "Is there a point to all of this?"

"Yes. My point is you take pride in the things you have. You don't let them fall apart or go hungry. I see your garden by the cabin has no weeds in it. On the way out here, I saw a lot of houses and barns. You'd be surprised how many people don't take the time to keep them in good condition. You, on the other hand, do."

"I still don't know what any of this has to do with you and your ma."

"Well, it stands to reason you'd treat me and my ma with the same care you treat your things. I could take my chances on another man by answering more ads, but I already know what I'd be getting here. Mr. Richie was wrong to lie about being you when he wrote me the missive. I won't argue that. But I have to admit you are as good as he made you sound."

"Carl and I aren't friends," he said. "There's been a feud going on between us for years."

"Then that says something, doesn't it? Even your enemy can find good things to say about you."

"He only said those things because he wanted you to come out here. He didn't say them because he believed them."

"Even so, he had no trouble coming up with things to say."

"Are you saying you want to marry me because of the way I sounded in that missive?" he asked, just to make sure he understood her.

"No. I came out here because of the missive. I want to marry you because I can tell you're the kind of man who'll be good to me and my ma." She hesitated for a moment then added, "Besides, I bet you could use a woman's help. Wouldn't it be nice to have someone cook and clean for you?"

Surprised by the sudden change in topic, he couldn't help but chuckle. "You just got through telling me what a great job I do taking care of everything, and then you say I could use someone around here to help me?"

"If you had some help, you wouldn't be doing everything alone."

"Well, yes, that stands to reason."

"So why not let me help you by marrying you?"

He studied her for a good minute. There was a spark in her that intrigued him. "It won't be an easy life."

"You've made that clear."

He glanced over at her mother who seemed just as sweet as the woman in front of him. Since he was a man, he wasn't nearly as vulnerable as they were. At least he could defend himself if he needed to, but they couldn't. In fact, they were naïve to the ways of the world.

"You said you have nowhere else to go?" he asked, just to make sure because if he could give them a way to escape the life he had to deal with, then it would be much better for them.

She shook her head. "My brother is generous to a fault, but we can't impose on him anymore. He'd take us in, but he doesn't make enough to support us and three children. He'll have the third soon. I tried to get a job, but no one wants to hire me because I'm too pretty. They're all afraid I'll get married and leave. And my mother is too old."

He almost laughed that people didn't want to hire her for such a simple reason. Instead of laughing, however, he asked, "So where were all the bachelors vying to marry you?"

"I come with my mother. Not many men are willing to take her in. We didn't live in a prosperous area. You have more than any of us did."

Compared to all Carl and Eric had, he didn't have much at all, but she had no way of knowing that, at least not with her brief time out here. "There's more to life than how much a man has," he said before he had time to think of the hypocrisy in his statement. How often had he'd argued with Carl over the property line, claiming he didn't have enough? "I mean that there's more than land and things that make marrying a good idea."

"Yes, I know. I also need someone kind enough to take my mother in and to be good to us."

"And you think I would do that?"

"You haven't been mean to me."

"You were afraid of me when I asked to see the letter," he reminded her. "Your hand was shaking."

"I wasn't afraid of you. I was afraid you'd tell me and my mother to go back to town without giving me a chance to explain the situation to you."

Oh.

"I grant you that I don't know you well enough to say we'd have a good marriage," she allowed. "I wasn't expecting to know such a thing anyway when I agreed to be a mail-order bride. But you do take what I want into consideration, and I know some men don't bother doing that with their wives. It stands to reason you'll be the same after we're married."

Since she was determined to pursue this course of action, he settled for a compromise. "I'll tell you what. The preacher doesn't come by this place except for once a month. You and your mother are welcome to stay in the same room. Then you can see what life with me will be like."

He was sure she'd be running on the next stagecoach that pulled into town once she realized just how hard life was out here, especially for a woman who was used to a big city among her own kind, but let her figure that out on her own. "When the preacher arrives, if you still want to stay here, I'll marry you."

"Thank you."

He wasn't so sure she'd be thanking him once she realized how much hardship she'd just asked for, but he figured she'd learn her mistake soon enough. "I'll bring your trunks into the house, and you can put your things away."

She nodded.

Deciding that was the end of their conversation, he went to get the trunks.

Chapter Four

It didn't take long for Phoebe and her mother to put their things away, but she didn't realize her hands were shaking until she closed the last drawer in the armoire. At one time, it had belonged to someone. Otherwise, it wouldn't be in this room, ready for use. There was also a bed her and her mother would share. She guessed a woman—perhaps Abe's mother—had lived in this cabin.

For all she knew, he'd built it for his mother. Or maybe his father had built it for his mother, though the two had never married. She wouldn't know the details unless she asked, and she felt she'd asked him too much already.

"At least you have a chance to get to know him before you marry him," her mother said.

Though her mother whispered, Phoebe glanced at the closed door, wondering if Abe could hear them. She went over to the small window and saw he was outside talking to Eric. Relieved, she turned back to her mother. "We can speak freely. He's not in the cabin." She went over to the bed and sat down, taking a moment to steady her nerves before continuing. "I didn't expect to be this nervous."

Her mother sat beside her and drew her in for a comforting hug. "Up to now, all we've been thinking of is making it through the trip."

She nodded. That was probably it. She settled her head on her mother's shoulder. "Do you think I made the right decision?"

"I don't see what other choice you had."

She swallowed her tears. "I wish he'd posted the ad instead of Carl. This would be much easier if he had."

"Yes, it would be." Her mother squeezed her shoulders. "I wish we had a rock in our purses when we hit him. He got off too easy, if you ask me."

She couldn't help but chuckle. "He did." She straightened up and wiped away a couple of tears that refused to stay at bay. "What was he thinking by doing something so horrible? He had to have known he was putting us and Abe in a difficult situation."

"Some people don't care who they hurt. All they care about is themselves. That Carl Richie is one of them."

"At least we know who to avoid when we go to town." She blinked back more tears. "Though it's not much of a town, is it?"

"We knew we'd have to give up a lot to live out West. But I will say this place is bigger than I thought it'd be. We could have fit us and your brother's family in here comfortably."

"That's true. It's one of the nicest places I've ever seen." She paused then asked, "Do you think that means Abe's a good man? I mean, he takes care of his things."

"Yes, I think he'll be good to you."

"I suppose it's just a matter of getting to know him. Then maybe I won't feel so nervous."

"Why don't you go out there and see if he needs help?"

Phoebe glanced out the window. Eric was no longer there. Her gaze went to the roof where Abe was laying something out. Would she get in his way? Would he tell her if she was? She supposed there was only one way to find out, and now that she was done helping her mother unpack, she had nothing else to do. Besides, maybe if she let him know she was willing to help, he'd feel better about having her and her mother here.

Her mother yawned, and Phoebe suddenly realized how much the days of travel had exhausted the poor woman. Phoebe fluffed the small pillow on the bed.

"I'll go out there and offer to help," she told her mother. "Lie down. You must be tired."

"Sometimes I miss being young. Don't take it for granted you can go out there and help him right after a long trip."

"I won't." After her mother settled onto the bed, Phoebe placed her hand on her arm and smiled. "I'm glad you're here."

Her mother clasped her hand over hers and squeezed it. "Everything will be alright. Just remember to see the good in things." With a contented sigh, she closed her eyes.

Phoebe waited for a moment, giving herself a chance to gather her courage, then left the room. She didn't know if Abe would welcome her out there or not. He had tried to dissuade her from marrying him. Maybe she should have explained everything to her mother, but in the end, all she said was that he offered to let them stay and see if marriage would benefit them both.

It took her a full two minutes before she was able to leave the house. It had proved to be a good hiding place, at least temporarily. But really, she couldn't hide there forever. Sooner or later, she had to see him.

She stepped onto the porch and softly shut the door. There were two rocking chairs, just as there had been two beds in the cabin. One chair must have been for his mother. The other must have been for him. He'd said his parents hadn't been married. Did that mean he didn't know his father? She hadn't dared to ask, nor did she think she'd have the nerve to do so. Not any time soon anyway. She'd just met him. While she intended to marry him, they had a ways to go before she'd find out the details about his past. She, on the other hand, had nothing to hide. He could ask her anything, and she'd answer him.

But that was neither here nor there. Before they were ready to talk about their past, they'd be better off getting to know each other, as her mother had suggested. She took a deep breath and released it. A breeze rustled the tree branches. Except for that and the occasional neighing and mooing from the animals, she didn't hear a thing. What a difference it was from Cincinnati. It was so quiet here. She didn't know if she'd ever get used to it, but she did enjoy the expanse of land which sloped gently down the hillside, and she liked the trees that were all around her, giving her a sense of privacy she'd never really had.

The sound of a hammer hitting a nail brought her attention back to Abe, who was pounding something on the roof. She swallowed the lump in her throat. She'd come out here to offer him a helping hand, and that's exactly what she'd do.

Acting braver than she felt, she headed down the porch steps and crossed the distance to the barn. He didn't notice her. At least, he didn't give any indication he noticed her.

"Abe?" she called out once she reached the ladder.

He stopped hammering and glanced down at her. "Do you need something?"

"No. Mother and I are fine. I came out to see if you needed help."

"Help?"

Noting the bewildered tone in his voice, she said, "Well, you're on top of the barn repairing the roof. I might not know much about fixing things, but I can offer my assistance. Just tell me what to do, and I'll do it."

He didn't answer right away, and she couldn't tell if he'd heard her or not over the rustling trees around them. But then, he said, "I could use some more nails."

"I'll be happy to bring them up. Where are they?"

"On the shelf over the worktable in the barn. It's right by the window."

"I'll be right up."

Without waiting for him to respond, she hurried into the barn. A horse neighed at her, almost causing her to bump into the worktable. She had to get a hold of herself. Yes, it was natural to be nervous. Any woman in her situation would be nervous. So much depended on how the next couple of weeks went.

Taking a moment to regain her composure, she scanned the barn. A horse was in one of the stalls, and there was a cow in the other. Two other stalls were empty, having just been swept out. There were hooks along the walls with rakes and shovels and other items hanging on them. Then there was a section in the corner with a saddle. Her gaze went up to the loft. She had no idea what he had up there. But as her gaze swept the ceiling, she could see the hole he was repairing. At the moment, he had resumed his hammering, reminding her he needed more nails.

She found the tin cup he'd mentioned and grabbed it. She climbed the ladder, careful to keep a firm grip on the cup as she did so. When she reached the roof, he put his hammer down and crossed the short distance to her.

"Thanks," he said, taking it.

He scooted back to the small hole.

He probably expected her to go back down the ladder and return to the house, but she decided to join him. Never once in Ohio did she think she'd ever be so bold. He hadn't invited her to come up on the roof, after all. But if she was going to marry him, she couldn't spend her entire life hiding from him.

She had to lift her skirt in order to get on the roof. Thankfully, he wasn't even looking in her direction, or else he would have seen her face flush a brighter shade of red from exposing so much of her legs.

Once she was presentable, she sat near him and asked, "What happened to the roof?"

He jerked, and she was surprised he hadn't heard her. She didn't think she'd been that quiet. "Do you mind if I'm up here?" she finally asked when he didn't say anything.

He blinked for a moment then shook his head. "No. I just thought you and your mother would be busy unpacking."

"Oh, we're done. I came out because there's nothing else to do. My mother is resting." She shrugged. "I don't like to sit around when there's work to be done."

"Well, this isn't the kind of work for a lady."

"I know, but I can help." She gestured to the cup of nails beside him. "I got those."

He let out a soft chuckle, and she couldn't help but note how nice he looked when he smiled. "I can't think of anything else for you to do."

She brought her knees up to her chest, hugging them. "Can I keep you company?"

He didn't answer right away. In fact, he looked down at the hammer and nails in this hand. Then, after a long moment, he returned his gaze to her. "You're a talker, aren't you?"

"A what?"

"A talker. You like to be around people. You don't like being alone. Am I right?"

"I don't like to be the center of attention, but I enjoy time with family and friends." When he didn't respond, she asked, "Are you the type who prefers to be alone?"

"I don't mind being alone. Sometimes it's better to be alone than be in a group and realize you're all alone."

Her eyebrows furrowed at his meaning. "How is that possible?"

He shook his head. "A pretty, white lady like you wouldn't know."

Trying not to let the fact that he called her pretty deter her from figuring out what he meant, she said, "My experience with people has been limited. I admit that. But I'd still like to know how that's possible."

He let out a long sigh. "Just because you are in a room full of people, it doesn't mean those people want you there. Sometimes they consider you to be an inconvenience. Sometimes you have to fight to be heard. It's good you'll never know what I'm talking about."

He turned his attention back to hammering the nail into the roof, and she struggled with knowing what to say next. Finally, she ventured, "I'm sorry you have to go through that."

He stopped pounding the nail. "It doesn't bother me. I'm used to it."

His comment made her wonder how much he'd been through, how often he felt left out. But she sensed it wasn't the time to press him on this. She'd only met him an hour ago. Deciding it might be best to change the topic, she scanned the property. There were trees throughout his land, and the buildings were on a slight incline. But further down, she caught sight of a stream just beyond a row of newly planted trees. When she looked up, above the trees, she caught sight of mountains in the background.

"You have a beautiful view," she said.

"It's alright."

"Alright? It's amazing. I've never seen such beauty."

He gestured to the stream with his hammer. "You see that area over there?"

"Yes."

"That should be mine, but Carl has staked it as if it belongs to him. And you want to know why? Because he thinks whatever he wants is his. He has no respect for other people's things."

To her surprise, he set the hammer and nails down and scooted over to her. He pushed his black hair over his shoulder.

"That area belonged to my uncle before he died," he continued. "He and my mother were forced out of their tribe when the white man came for the gold in Georgia. He built this place with his own two hands. Then he died and left my mother everything. After that, Carl's father felt it was his right to take the stream and twenty acres on the other side of it." He motioned back to the area surrounded by trees. "That's what white men do. They see something and they take it. They don't care if it already belongs to someone or not. Then they have the nerve to act as if we're wrong for wanting them to get off our land. You know what Carl wants with that land?"

Of course, she didn't, which made it ironic he even asked the question. But since he seemed to want her to speak, she obliged him. "What does he want?"

"Gold."

She didn't know what he expected her to say. In Ohio, these things weren't important. She'd only heard a little about gold rushes out West, but it'd never concerned her so she dismissed the small tidbits she'd heard. Apparently, the whole thing was important out here, and she had a nagging suspicion she was going to learn a lot more about it in the years to come.

Abe let out a long sigh and rubbed his forehead. "I'm sorry. I shouldn't be troubling you with all of this. It's not your fault. I know you're white, but you had nothing to do with it. Sometimes I have to remind myself not all white people are bad."

With a sinking feeling in her heart, Phoebe turned her attention back to the mountains. She didn't know much of his past, but from what she gathered, things hadn't been very pleasant for him. And this would undoubtedly affect how things were going to be between them.

He glanced at her then to the hole in the roof. "I should get back to work."

She nodded and decided it might be in her best interest to get back into the house. She didn't think there was anything she could say or do to make things better. At least not right now. Besides, her mother would be getting up soon, and when she did, Phoebe wanted to help her with the evening meal.

Chapter Five

When Abe was done repairing the roof and feeding the animals, he went into the cabin. He'd gotten used to coming into a dim room, which was either hot or cold, depending on the weather. But this time when he opened the door, there was a breeze blowing in through the open windows and the smell of biscuits and stew were in the air.

The two women were busy setting the table, so they didn't notice him. He took a moment to watch them. For a moment, he was reminded of the times he'd come in from finishing the chores to see his mother making dinner. The place hadn't been the same since she died.

Phoebe and her mother stopped talking and looked over at him. Feeling self-conscious, he gave them a nod as a greeting and shut the door. He wiped the sweat from his brow, trying to think of what he could say to make things less awkward.

None of them asked to be stuck in this situation. Carl had written the ad, pretending to be him. Phoebe and her mother were probably as nervous about this new setup as he was. But since he was the man, he figured it was up to him to say something first.

He cleared his throat. "It smells good in here." *Wonderful, Abe. Just come out and state the obvious.*

"Thank you," Phoebe's mother said. "Why don't you sit on down, and we'll start eating in a moment."

Since she patted the chair next to her, he went over to the chair. He glanced at Phoebe, but she was gathering the biscuits onto a tray. He swallowed. The last time that tray had been used, his mother had put tea on it to entertain his father. She had wanted so much to please him that she had only the best things out whenever he came over. To this day, he didn't understand her mindless devotion to him.

"I hope you like stew," Phoebe's mother said.

Turning his attention to her, he nodded. "Yes, I do."

"I couldn't help but notice your garden when we came in," she continued as she put the large pot in the middle of the table. "Back in Cincinnati, we didn't have room to grow anything. Not even a small plot. Out here, though, you have so much space, and I notice you make good use of it."

"It is the way of my people to use everything we're given," he said. "To waste anything is wrong."

"Your people?"

"Ma," Phoebe quickly said, "where did you put the tea punch?"

Her mother's gaze went to the worktable. "Oh, over there, I think."

While Phoebe went to get the pitcher, he glanced at her. Did she interrupt her mother on purpose? Wasn't she the least bit curious which tribe he came from?

Phoebe returned with the pitcher. "Have you ever had tea punch before, Abe?"

"No, I can't say I have."

"It's a recipe we used to make quite a bit back home. I couldn't help but notice your tea bags. I thought it'd be a good way to use them. I hope that's alright. Would you rather have regular tea?"

"No." He didn't want to ever drink tea again. It only reminded him of the white men who'd forced his people off their land and, in so doing, forced his mother and uncle out here. He wasn't even sure he wanted to drink tea punch. But he had a difficult time disappointing an old woman. If nothing else, he'd do it out of respect for her. "I look forward to trying it," he finally said.

She smiled, and he felt better on her behalf. She went through a lot of trouble to make this meal with her daughter. The least he could do was eat it.

Soon, they began the meal. For a good five minutes, they ate in silence. Phoebe, who was sitting across from him, refused to look at him. Earlier that day, she'd made an impassioned plea for him to marry her. And considering the fact that she made it a point to come out to the barn and sit on the roof while he worked, he had no idea why she chose to avoid eye contact with him now.

Women were difficult to figure out. He wasn't likely to understand Phoebe any more than he understood his own mother. He forced his attention back to his food, choosing to listen as Phoebe's mother told him about all the places they'd been on their way here. Apparently, they'd started out on a train, and after making a transfer to a different one, they spent the night in a town whose name he couldn't pronounce. From there, they took the stagecoach, which ended up being an eight-day journey.

"The important thing is we're here now," her mother finished with a wide smile. "You got a real nice place, Abe. It's much better than some we saw along the way. Even the houses in town weren't quite as nice, though I recall the yellow one being adorable." She took a breath then asked, "Is the tea punch satisfactory?"

Surprised she'd stopped her discourse on the trip to ask the question, he didn't answer right away. After taking a moment to clear his throat, he nodded. "It's much better than plain tea." Her eyebrows furrowed, so he clarified, "I like it."

"Oh good," she replied, looking relieved. "There's so much tea I didn't want to waste it." She stood up and took his plate. "Don't mind me and Phoebe. We'll clean up. You go on and do whatever you need to, right Phoebe?"

Though Phoebe nodded, she still didn't look over at him. She only got up and helped her mother collect the dishes.

Deciding he had nothing to contribute, he rose to his feet and headed for the door. He might be better off getting chores done early. Then when he got back, he'd go to bed. It was awkward enough sitting through a meal with the two women. He didn't need to sit out in the main room with them.

Just as he reached the door, her mother called out to him. He turned back toward her, and she walked to him, moving faster than he thought possible for a woman her age.

When she stopped in front of him, she put her hand on his arm and gave him a reassuring smile. "You can call me Viv. My name is Vivian, but my family and friends call me Viv."

"Alright," he replied, not sure what else he was supposed to say. Except for maybe one thing. "The meal was good."

"I'm glad you think so. Whatever Phoebe and I can do to make things easier for you, let us know." She paused for a moment, glanced over at Phoebe who was washing dishes, and said, "Give her time. She's always been shy around new people. She'll come around to talking more as she gets comfortable." She patted his arm again then went back to help her daughter.

That was funny. Phoebe hadn't struck him as shy earlier that day. Oh well. He had better things to do than wonder why she'd been so quiet during the meal. He opened the door and stepped outside.

On a whim, he glanced back. There was no doubt how close Phoebe and her mother were. Viv said something that made Phoebe chuckle. Phoebe had a nice laugh. He guessed it would be even better when she burst out into laughter. The sunlight streaming in through the window settled on her hair, making it shine like the gold so many white men valued. Valued so much they drove out anyone in their way so they could get to it. He swallowed the bitter thought, shut the door, and went to the barn.

"PHOEBE, WHAT'S WRONG?" her mother asked as soon as Abe left.

Phoebe should have known her mother would pick up that some-thing was wrong. Well, not wrong, really. Just...difficult. And she didn't know how to adequately explain that to her.

Since her mother was standing right next to her and giving her that all-too-familiar look that insisted Phoebe had to tell her, she did.

"Alright," Phoebe relented, putting the dish in the bucket and turn-ing to her. "This is going to be harder than I expected. Abe thinks a lot of white people are evil."

"Evil?"

"He didn't use those exact words. He said that white men take things from Indians, and because of this, it's hard to trust them."

Her mother took a moment to consider her words before answer-ing. "Well, I can't say I know much about Indians and how they've been treated. Did someone do something to Abe because he's got Indi-an blood in him?"

"Carl's claimed some acreage and the stream Abe said is rightfully his."

"The stream? You mean the one Carl wrote in that missive saying Abe owned?"

Phoebe nodded.

Her mother shook her head. "Given the fact that Carl pretended to be Abe, it shouldn't surprise me he lied about the stream."

"But the stream and land with it is Abe's. Abe's uncle came here and claimed it, fair and square, before Carl's father came out here. I think Carl's father just wanted the gold."

"I've heard of gold rushes. Only a few strike it rich. Everyone else ends up worse off than they were before. Is Carl's father still alive?"

"I don't think so since Carl owns the land and stream now. At least, Carl says he owns it."

It was hard to know what the truth was, but if she had to guess, she'd say Abe was right. Abe, after all, hadn't been deceitful enough to send a mail-order bride ad in another man's name. Phoebe glanced at the dishes in the bucket and picked up the wet cloth she'd been using to wash them. But instead of resuming the wash, she only stared at the cloth.

"Do you think Abe can look beyond the fact we're white?" Phoebe finally asked her mother.

"Oh, I don't see why the fact we're white should make a difference."

"I wouldn't think so either, except if he is having trouble trusting white people, then where does that leave us?"

"You should ask him."

"I can't do that!"

"Why not? You're going to be married to him. If you can ask anyone anything, it should be the person you're married to."

Her mother was right, of course. Phoebe couldn't argue the point. But she barely knew him. How could she come right out and ask him if he trusted them? Besides, didn't it take time for people to trust each other, regardless of their skin color?

"Phoebe," her mother began, "is that why you interrupted me tonight when I asked Abe about his tribe? Were you afraid it'd remind him we're white?"

"He was upset when he was talking about white men stealing things from others. I thought he might go into that again, and it would be hard to enjoy a meal with that as the topic of conversation."

"But not everything in life is pleasant," her mother tenderly told her. "There are bad things that happen. I don't mind if Abe tells me about them. You don't have to shelter me. We've had it better than most. I don't have to know what's happened to his tribe to know this. Your father and Phillip took good care of us. And I have a feeling Abe will do the same. We've been blessed far more than most."

Noting her mother's yawn, Phoebe said, "Why don't you go on to bed? I'll finish up the dishes."

"Tomorrow, I should be able to do more."

"You've done a lot today. The trip wore me out, too, but I'm younger and can handle it better."

"Youth does have its advantages." She placed her hand on Phoebe's arm and squeezed it. "It'll work out. Just give it time. Being a bride soon, you're likely to have doubts. Sometimes you have to think with your head, and you and I both know Abe is a good man. Don't give fear a foothold."

Her mother released her arm and retreated to the bedroom. With a sigh, Phoebe turned back to the dishes and picked one up. As she ran the soapy cloth over it, she dared a peak out the window.

Abe was leading a horse toward the barn. He gave it a friendly pat on the neck, and though she couldn't hear him, she saw him talking to it. The horse, as if understanding him, neighed and shook its head.

Releasing her breath, she turned her attention back to the dish. Alright. So she had to talk to Abe. Only then would her doubts be settled. But how on earth was she going to do it?

Chapter Six

The next morning, Abe tapped the top of the pitchfork. Things had been just as awkward at breakfast as they had been the previous evening at supper, and he didn't know what to do about it. Had it not been for Phoebe's mother telling him about her son and his family, the tension would have been unbearable. Something needed to change. He just didn't know what.

The horses neighed at him, so he turned his attention back to the pile of hay in front of him. He dug his pitchfork into it, gathered a good amount of hay, and set it in their troughs. Content, they stopped neighing at him and began eating. If only women were as easy to figure out as horses. His mother had been a mystery to him. Now Phoebe would be one as well.

Once he was finished with the horses, he milked the cow. He retrieved the pail full of fresh milk and took it to the house. Phoebe was washing dishes while her mother was rocking in his mother's favorite chair. It was strange to see someone in his mother's chair, but he figured someone might as well get some use out of it.

He went over to Phoebe and showed her the pail. "Where do you want it?"

"Um," Phoebe glanced around her then pointed to the worktable, "over there will be fine."

He nodded and set it down.

"Abe," her mother spoke up, sitting straight up in the chair. "I was wondering, how often do you make a trip into town to get supplies?"

He shrugged. "Once a month. Maybe once every two months. It depends on the weather." And if he had any business to do in town. "Do you need to go there?"

"There are a couple things I wouldn't mind having. I get bored just sitting around doing nothing, and more than that, I'd like to make myself useful. Got anything you need me to mend or sew?"

"Oh, well..." It'd been a long time since he last checked the clothes that needed mending. "I think there's two shirts and one pair of denims that are coming apart."

"Good! I'll be happy to make them as good as new. Why don't you and Phoebe run on to town and collect supplies for me?"

Phoebe glanced up from the pan she'd been washing. "You don't want to come along?"

"No," her mother said. "I'm not fully rested from our trip." She looked at Abe. "We packed light. You wouldn't mind it if she bought a couple items to pretty herself up, would you?"

When Phoebe's gaze went to him, he said, "You're welcome to get whatever you need."

Of all the things people could say about him, withholding things a woman needed wasn't going to be one of them. While Phoebe and her mother were there, he'd see to their needs.

"We'll leave in thirty minutes," he added then left the cabin to get the horses ready.

He suspected her mother had ulterior motives for sending him and Phoebe into town. Most likely, Phoebe knew it, too. He wasn't exactly looking forward to sitting with Phoebe for nearly an hour, but he figured it wouldn't hurt to get some things resolved. They would have to spend a couple weeks in the same house until the next stagecoach came back. Surely, they could come to an understanding that would allow them to live peaceably.

He got the horses hitched to the wagon before the half hour was up, and he fully expected to wait for her to come out, much like he'd have to wait for his mother, who insisted on making sure she looked as beautiful as possible in case they ran into his father while in town. Even now, Abe grimaced in irritation. Why did she degrade herself that way? No wonder Carl thought he could walk all over him. He'd watched his father do it to Abe's mother his entire life.

The door to the cabin opened, and Abe's mind returned to the present. Phoebe had put her hat on, and she was sliding the ribbons of her drawstring purse up her arm. There was no doubt she was a pretty thing. She almost seemed too good for this place. A bigger house with far more land would have suited her better. Why hadn't any of the white men back in Ohio taken an interest in her? Were men stupid over there?

Phoebe took a deep breath, squared her shoulders back, and marched toward him, much as a man would do when faced with a battle.

Despite the situation, a chuckle escaped Abe's throat. "I'm not going to hurt you. You have nothing to fear."

"That's not what I'm thinking," she said, seeming surprised by his comment.

"Then why do you look as if you're going to die?"

Her eyebrows furrowed and her steps slowed as she reached the wagon. "I don't have any reason to think I'm going to die."

He went over to her. "Well, something's on your mind." He held his hand out to her. "I'll help you in."

She bit her lower lip.

"If you want to get in yourself, you certainly may," he said, gesturing to the seat. "But that skirt's likely to give you some problems unless you lift it. Of course, if you lift it, I'm likely to see something I shouldn't."

At that, her face went bright red, and she thrust her hand out to him. He stared at her, not sure if he should laugh or be concerned. Something was troubling her. She hadn't been afraid of him when she asked him if she could stay, nor was she afraid when she brought the nails up to him while he was fixing the roof. He thought over the things he'd said or done that might have spooked her, but he couldn't think of anything.

After a moment, he took her hand and helped her into the wagon. When he made it to his side, he got in next to her and glanced her way. Again, she refused to look at him. Perhaps she worried about being alone on the trail with him. Maybe she thought he'd take advantage of the situation.

He unlocked the brakes and snapped the reins, encouraging the horses to move forward. She gasped and lost her balance. Leaning toward her, he put his arm around her waist and steadied her before she fell back.

"I thought you were familiar with wagons," he said.

"I-I am," she stammered as she finally found her balance. He released her, and she cleared her throat. "I just didn't expect the horses to go so fast, that's all."

She hadn't expected the horses to go so fast? He glanced at her to see if she was serious. Eric had brought her out on his wagon, and those horses were moving faster than his were.

Since her face was an even brighter shade of red than it'd been before, he decided to let the observation pass. Instead, he said, "There's no reason you should be afraid of me. I'm not going to do anything I shouldn't."

"I know," she replied, the slight waver in her voice betraying her.

"Phoebe, if we're going to be living in the same house until the stagecoach arrives, we can't dodge the issue. I don't know what happened, but ever since you went up on the barn roof to help me, you've been avoiding me. The next few weeks will go a lot smoother if you just come out and tell me why."

She took a deep breath. He thought for sure she wasn't going to say anything, and he was ready to give up when she said, "Alright. There is something troubling me."

Good. They were finally getting somewhere. "What is it?"

"Do you wish me and my mother weren't white?"

"No. You and your mother can't help being white."

"But if we were Indian, would we be better?"

Surprised by the question, he thought over his response before answering. "You and your mother are white, and since there's no changing it, I don't wish you and your mother were Indian. It just is what it is." When she frowned, he added, "I don't hate white people. There are some nice ones. Eric Johnson is one of them. There's Travis Martin, too. Granted, Travis keeps to himself, and because of that, he's never caused any trouble. But then you have the likes of Carl. Those types, unfortunately, outnumber the good ones. Most white people, especially the men, aren't any good. You can't trust them. If they're being nice, it's because they want something, and when that happens, you better watch your back."

"It's not fair of you to say that about all white people."

"I didn't say all white people. I said most, and I singled out the men, but some white women aren't so nice, either. Sure, they aren't out grabbing land and stealing goods from an Indian, but they act like anyone who isn't white is out to rape, murder, or steal from them. Watch the way the women act around me when we're in town. Then you'll see what I'm talking about."

"But you look white."

"I'm a half-breed. As far as they're concerned, I'm full-blooded Indian." He shook his head. "And more than that, I'm a bastard. Are you telling me in Ohio, the fine white people readily accept bastards?"

She shifted uncomfortably. "No. It's preferable if everyone is born in wedlock, even if there is a last minute wedding before the baby is born."

"Exactly. I have two things against me, and those are two things too many. Now, I don't blame you for any of this. You and your mother seem like nice women. I'm not going to hurt either one of you. All

I want is to live my life in peace, and I want what's rightfully mine. There's nothing wrong with that, is there?"

"No."

"Good. So maybe we can get along until it's time for you to leave on the next stagecoach."

"I already said I'm not leaving on it."

"By the time you see how things are in town, you'll change your mind."

She shook her head, but he decided she'd find out how right he was soon enough. Phoebe, he was quickly learning, had a stubborn streak in her. Once she set her mind to something, she did everything in her power to make it happen. But even a strong-willed woman wouldn't be able to stand against the majority of people in town.

"If nothing else," he continued, "it'd be nice to get along while you and your mother are here. Since you two are willing to stay with me, obviously you aren't like other white people. You don't need to worry I've lumped you in with them. I haven't. So, what do you say? Can we be friends?"

"Yes, we can."

"Thank you."

That was a relief. Maybe next time he offered to help her up in the wagon, she wouldn't flinch. It was bad enough he had to put up with the looks and whispers in town. He didn't need to get it with her, too. He turned his attention back to the path in front of them, and they rode the rest of the way in silence.

Chapter Seven

When they got to town, Phoebe thought it was even smaller than she'd remembered. The few people who were gathered outside had decided it was far more interesting to stare at her and Abe than to continue on in their conversations.

Ignoring them, she glanced at Abe. Could he really accept her and her mother since they weren't more like him? If she'd had some Indian blood in her, she suspected he would've accepted her right away. She *was* different from him, and she didn't know if he really could separate his feelings for the people in town from her and her mother.

But he'd asked her to give him a chance, and the least she could do was what he wanted. As he pulled the wagon up to the general store, he turned to her. "Do you know what you want, or are you going to look around?"

"My mother gave me a list of items she needs," she said, pulling it from the pocket of her skirt. "I thought I'd take a look around and see if I need anything." She cleared her throat. "Is there any food you'd like me to get while we're here?"

"I don't care as long as it's not any of Carl's. Avoid anything with the Richie label."

She nodded and waited for him to come over to her side of the wagon before getting down. If he hadn't made the comment about her skirt, she would have gotten down herself, but the last thing she needed to do was give any of the onlookers a show.

"I'm going to the post office and then the lumber store," Abe told her. "Afterwards, I'll come to the store to pay for the items. That way, we don't have to be in town any longer than we need to." He paused. "That is, unless you want me to go to the store with you."

"I've been to a store before," she told him, aware the people were still staring. "I know how to find things there."

"I didn't mean to imply you didn't. I just thought being new here..." He sighed. "Never mind. I'm sure whatever I say you'd only take it the wrong way."

As he started to head off, she asked, "What do you mean by that?"

With a glance around, he came back to her and lowered his voice. "I thought you wanted my help in there, that's all. Some items are pretty high, and I could reach them for you."

"Oh. Is there a ladder or something to step on to reach them?"

"Yes, but it's not always available."

She hadn't considered that. He made a good point. But since he was uncomfortable being in town and since the people were still staring at them, she decided it would be better to make things go as quickly as possible. "You go on ahead to the post office and lumber store. I'll go to the general store. If I see anything out of reach, I'll wait until you're there to get it."

He nodded in satisfaction and led her up the steps to the boardwalk. As they passed by two men lounging in a chair, one of them snickered. She looked his way, but he'd already turned his gaze to something across the street. Her eyebrows furrowed. What was the snickering about?

From beside her, Abe let out a sigh and opened the door. "I won't be long," he told her, gesturing to the interior of the general store.

She mumbled a thank you and went into the store. After the door closed behind her, she glanced back. The two men didn't talk to Abe, something she had expected, but they did chuckle and whisper something to each other as Abe headed to the post office. She'd thought Abe was exaggerating when he mentioned how things were in town. There might, however, be more truth to what he said than she'd been willing to accept.

"May I help you?" a man asked.

She turned and saw a thin man right in front of her. He had a handlebar mustache and looked to be in his mid-thirties. He was tall, too. Probably a good six feet and five inches in height.

"Um...yes." She unfolded the piece of paper her mother had written on then handed it to him. "These are some of them. I was going to browse the store to see what else I wanted."

He took the paper from her and scanned it. "How do you intend to pay?"

"I'm not going to pay. Abe Thomas is." She motioned in the direction of the post office. "He's over there right now, and then he'll go to the lumber store." When he frowned, she added, "But he'll be here after that."

"I see Carl got that mail-order bride for him after all," he said then went to grab a basket.

Maybe she shouldn't press the issue, but she couldn't help but blurt out, "You knew Carl posted a mail-order bride ad on Abe's behalf?"

"It's a small town. There's not much I don't know." He scanned the list again and began collecting the items written on it.

She followed him. "I don't understand. If you knew, then why didn't Abe know?"

"No one told him."

"Why not? Don't you think he had a right to know?"

"Little lady," he said, stopping to turn around and look down at her, "there are some things men have a right to, and when a half-breed bastard tries to take it, a distraction goes a long way."

A half-breed bastard? A distraction? What in the world was he talking about? "I don't understand. What does that have to do with Carl posting an ad and you not warning Abe?"

"Abe's not one of us," the man gently told her. "I can't blame Carl for what he did. Abe wasn't giving up."

"Giving up on what?"

"Carl has a right to the land he's on, and Abe's been interfering with that right. Carl figured with you here, Abe would have better things to do than to fight with him."

"Are you talking about the part of the land with a stream on it?"

He nodded. "Abe's lucky Carl's letting him stay in the cabin he currently occupies. You ought to remind Abe of that. It was Carl's father who owned that land to begin with."

"But isn't Carl's father also Abe's father?" The words flew out of her mouth before she had time to think over the wisdom of using them.

"Unless the son is legitimate, he has no claim to the inheritance."

She shut her mouth then, only because it became clear he was talking to her as if she were a child.

Fortunately, he turned back to filling the basket with items her mother had written on the paper, so she was spared from having to engage in any more conversation with him. She didn't know whether to be embarrassed or angry about the whole thing.

While the owner continued gathering the things, she browsed the other items he was selling, her enthusiasm at getting something new diminished significantly. In Ohio, she'd loved to spend time in stores, picking out things she'd love to take home. She couldn't afford to take everything she'd wanted, of course, but she'd made it a habit of pausing and imagining what it'd be like to own the item of interest. Such fantasies eluded her now. She wasn't sure she wanted to ever come back here again, let alone have Abe buy them for her today.

The door opened, and thinking it was Abe, she looked over at the doorway. She hid her disappointment. It was one of the men, who'd been staring at her and Abe as she came into the store. No doubt, he was just as pleasant as the owner, what with the way he snickered and all.

No, she must not think that way. It wasn't fair to make assumptions based on her conversation with the owner. She'd give everyone a chance. Perhaps the man hadn't snickered at her or Abe. Perhaps, he'd been thinking of something else. Or maybe he had something stuck between his teeth he was trying to dislodge with his tongue. There could be many reasons for what he did.

As it turned out, the man came over to her. "Howdy there, Miss," he greeted, tipping his hat.

She stepped away from him, trying not to be obvious about the way he repulsed her. He smelled like he hadn't had a bath in over a month, and worse, there was alcohol on his breath. "Good afternoon," she mumbled then forced her attention to the row of staple items in front of her.

He came around her other side, an action which boxed her into the corner, unless she chose to go around him, but that would require her to touch him, and she didn't much care for that option.

"I heard you came in yesterday," he said, probably smiling in what he thought was a charming manner.

She swallowed and concentrated on keeping her voice steady. "Yes." Maybe if she didn't give him more than simple answers, he'd go away.

"I also heard Carl wrote a mail-order bride ad and sent you to Abe Thomas."

He took a step toward her, and she backed up, her hip hitting something on the shelf that wobbled. She glanced at the owner, who didn't seem interested enough in what was happening to look their way. She swallowed. What was wrong with these people? Didn't anyone offer help when they saw a lady who needed it?

"Please, sir," she began, "I need to go outside and get a breath of fresh air. Will you kindly step aside so I can get to the door?"

"Actually, I was thinking we should get better acquainted," he replied, stepping even closer to her.

With nowhere else to go, she could only press her back up against the shelves. She glanced at the owner, hoping he'd do something to help her, but the owner was taking the basket of goods to the counter. He had to know what was going on. Why wasn't he doing something to stop this?

"Name's Enoch," the man said, making a show of looking her up and down, his gaze settling on her breasts.

She crossed her arms to block his view of them. "Enoch," she swallowed, "I don't know who you think I am, but I'm not that kind of woman."

"Come now, *Miss* Durbin. Don't play games with me." In a lower voice, he said, "You're living with a half-breed. You can't tell me he hasn't enjoyed you."

He reached for her behind, and she slapped his hand away. "He most certainly hasn't! Abe is a gentleman. My mother and I slept in one room, and he slept in another."

Enoch threw back his head and laughed. "You tell some entertaining stories, Miss Durbin, but I'm a man and there's no way Abe has you out there without enjoying what you have to offer."

In a bold move, he pressed himself up against her and tried to grab her breast. Gasping, she made an attempt to push him away, but he was much too strong for her.

"Sir," she called out to the owner, "help me!"

"He ain't going to help you," Enoch whispered as he lowered his head to kiss her neck. "He hates Abe too much." He kissed her again.

"No!" She hit him, but it made no difference. The brute was much too big.

Suddenly, he was off of her. In one fluid motion, she saw him fly across the room until he crashed into a display of pots and pans in the middle of the store. He landed on the floor, and Abe pulled out a gun and pointed it at him.

"What's the meaning of this?" the owner asked, finally doing something.

Phoebe gritted her teeth, wanting to throw something at the owner. Unfortunately, she was trembling too much to grab anything.

Abe glared at the owner. "You got nerve, Benny. You were going to let this piece of filth rape her right here in your store?"

"You kill him and they'll hang you," Benny said, not even having the decency to apologize for not trying to stop Enoch.

Abe lowered his weapon, so it was aimed at Enoch's crotch. Then he cocked the gun.

"No, no!" Enoch covered his crotch, tears springing to his eyes. "Not there. Anywhere but there."

"I forbid you to fire that gun, half-breed," Benny snapped.

"You're nothing better than a pig," Abe spat on Enoch and then kicked at the man's hands, effectively striking his crotch in the same blow.

The man cried and fell onto his side, curling up and holding himself.

"You ever touch her again," Abe said, "and I'll make sure that wife of yours doesn't have any more children."

Wife? Phoebe's eyes widened. Enoch was married?

Abe turned to Benny and pointed the gun at him. "You listen here. I don't care what you and the others say about me. But you will never treat Phoebe that way ever again. You hear me? Because whether they hang me or not, I'll shoot you. By the way, you won't be charging us for these items because of what you were going to let Enoch do."

Benny opened his mouth to protest, and Abe fired the gun. Phoebe hid her eyes, but then peeked between her fingers. The bullet had gone right past Benny's ear and hit the sack of flour on the shelf behind him. No doubt, Abe was warning Benny. There was no way he could miss a shot that close.

Benny clenched his teeth. After a tense moment, he grabbed the basket and dumped it at Abe's feet. "Get out and don't come back."

Abe nodded at Phoebe. "Take it."

Despite the fact her legs were wobbly, she hurried to the basket and picked it up.

Abe then glanced between Benny and Enoch. "If you or anyone else steps on my property to do any harm, you'll live to regret it. I might not get away with killing any of you, but there's other ways to make you suffer. Go to the wagon, Phoebe. I'll be right behind you."

Phoebe was too scared to stay there, so she bolted on out of there. She threw the basket in the back of the wagon and scrambled up into the seat, lowering the hat over her forehead and avoiding eye contact with anyone who happened to be watching.

Her heart was hammering so loudly in her chest she thought it might burst. She didn't realize she was trembling until she noticed her shaky hands. Crossing her arms, she was able to steady them.

Things couldn't have transpired the way she thought they did in there. That horrible Enoch hadn't been trying to grope her right in public, and worse, the owner hadn't really ignored the whole thing. None of it was decent at all. In all her time in Cincinnati, she'd never heard of such a thing happening to a woman. Sure, she'd heard of places called brothels where men used women for pleasure, but that kind of thing wasn't supposed to happen in a general store.

She heard the door of the general store open and saw Abe coming out, his expression dark. He slammed the door and paused to look around. Curious, she followed his gaze, noting that six people were staring at him. She couldn't be sure, but she thought his expression went darker, as if he was daring any of them to confront him.

One of the women hurried off down the dirt road and scrambled into another building. The men, however, weren't so easily dissuaded and only continued staring at him.

After a long moment, Abe went over to the wagon and got up on the seat. Phoebe noted he was still holding his gun as he released the brake. Was someone going to shoot them? He had to think it was a possibility if he hadn't put it back in his holster.

She gulped and closed her eyes. If gunfire was going to erupt, she didn't want to see it. Better just let it be quick and over with. She gripped the edge of her seat, sure something bad was going to happen at any minute.

But the only thing that happened was the wagon moving forward, bouncing her as they went over the uneven road. It wasn't until a few minutes passed before Abe told her she could open her eyes, and even then she was afraid to.

"Phoebe," Abe said, "we're out of town. No one's going to harm us."

She took a deep breath then opened them, sure that someone would jump out at them from the trees lining their path. But no one did such a thing. She glanced behind them, assured they really were safe. She exhaled, her grip on the seat relaxing.

"I had no idea that was going to happen," Abe said. "If I'd known, I wouldn't have left you alone. I'm sorry. I know they don't like me, but I thought you were safe because you're white. None of the other white women have to worry about that kind of thing around here."

"Why didn't you have Enoch and Benny arrested?" Phoebe demanded.

"I'm a half-breed. That makes me less than human. Enoch and Benny are white. It doesn't matter what they do. The sheriff wouldn't have done anything. Not when it's two white men's word against mine."

"What if I back up your story? We can go back and hold them responsible for what they did." She gestured back to the town.

"It's not that simple. I didn't realize your association with me would make you vulnerable. If I'd known, I never would have agreed to take you and your mother in. I would have insisted Eric do it. But apparently, they all assume you're spending time in my bed. We're not mar-

ried, and I'm a half-breed. I should have known that was a bad combination. They think you're no better than I am." He shook his head.
"Look, Phoebe, you have to get out of here when the stagecoach comes.
You can't live this kind of life. I'll give you and your mother money and
send you back to Ohio. I doubt you'll end up with another half-breed.
Chances are, you'll find a good, white man who'll take care of you and
your mother, and next time, he'll be the one who actually posts the ad.
If we do this now, you can get back before the weather turns bad and
travel is impossible."

She didn't know how to respond to that. What he said made sense.
It was the logical thing to do. Maybe she should do it. Her mother had
survived the trip out here. She could survive the one back to Ohio.
Then next year when they tried again, maybe that one would work out.

If she couldn't venture into town without someone trying to hurt
her, how could she ever be safe? How could her mother be safe? She
closed her eyes and tried to block out all the bad from her mind, even
if it was a temporary reprieve. She'd think better once the emotions
weren't so fresh.

Chapter Eight

That evening as Abe was tending to the animals, he heard horse's hooves hitting the dirt road leading to his property. He dropped the pitchfork and grabbed his gun. He rounded the edge of the barn and peered around the side that gave him the best view of the road. He didn't think anyone would come onto his land to hurt him or Phoebe while it was light out, but who knew what to expect?

The last thing he'd thought that lowlife Enoch would do was try to force himself upon her—and right there in the general store where anyone could see him. His grip tightened on his gun. If it was either Enoch or Benny, he'd put a bullet right between their eyes. He had every right to defend his home and the people who lived here.

But as it turned out, the visitor was Eric Johnson. Breathing a sigh of relief, he tucked the gun into the holster and came out of hiding. "Over here," he called out.

Eric turned in his direction and headed over to him. "I heard what happened in town," Eric said as he got down from his horse.

"Don't tell me you came to arrest me for defending Phoebe," Abe replied. "Enoch got lucky. I could have done worse than kick him."

"I didn't come to arrest you. I came to ask why you didn't bring the matter to my attention. Don't you think I want to know if someone tries to rape a woman?"

Abe shook his head. "It's not that easy."

"No?"

"No. It was my word against Enoch's and Benny's. They would have both denied what happened."

"It doesn't matter what they would have said. I would've believed you."

"Maybe, but I didn't want you to risk your reputation by siding with a half-breed. The others in town wouldn't like it."

"I keep telling you I don't care what they think," Eric said. "I'm the sheriff in this place, and I've vowed to protect everyone in this town."

"Yes, well, protecting me could mean they come to your place ready to chase you on out of here or set fire to your house to teach you a lesson."

"Let them try it. I'm not scared of them."

"My uncle said that, too, until he got shot."

"Enoch and Benny might know people, but I do, too." Eric rubbed the back of his neck. "Things aren't as bad as you think they are, Abe. Not anymore. Anyway, I came to tell you I took care of it. Enoch and Benny are in jail."

"You arrested them?" Abe asked, not believing his ears.

"Of course, I did. It was the right thing to do."

Abe didn't know how to respond to that. The last thing he'd expected was for anyone to actually do anything about Enoch and Benny. Nothing had been done when his mother and uncle had suffered from the hands of the townsfolk. But then, that was before Eric came to live here.

"Thank you," Abe finally said.

"You're welcome," Eric replied. "How is Phoebe taking it?"

"Not well. She hasn't said anything since we got back."

"I'll talk to her. Maybe knowing they're in jail will help set her mind at ease."

"Wait," Abe said as Eric turned to go to the house. "I want you to do something for me. If someone comes after me for the fact that Enoch and Benny are in jail, will you keep Phoebe and her mother safe?"

"It's not going to come to that, Abe."

"How can you guarantee that?"

"Because I'm in charge around here, and I don't tolerate injustice, that's how. I understand what my predecessor was like. He looked the other way whenever it didn't benefit him to stand for what's right. But I care about everyone. I want this place to be safe."

"They might not come after me. They might go after you if you keep defending a half-breed."

"I'm not defending a half-breed. I'm defending a human being. What happened to your mother and uncle wasn't fair, but I wasn't here to stop it. I'm here now."

"You better be careful," Abe said. As much as he admired and respected Eric, he was afraid the man was going to get himself killed.

"I will be. No one really cares for Benny or Enoch. Benny's been cheating people out of a fair deal, and Enoch's a drunkard. They might be white, but believe me, people see what they're like, and no one is going to be sorry to see them get what's coming to them. I've never been able to catch them doing anything I could arrest them for, but I got them today. I'm keeping my eyes out on a couple others who haven't done this town a bit of good. People are afraid to do anything about the lawlessness around here. That's why it's been allowed to go on for so long. But I'm here now, and I'm going to give the good people of this town a reason to fight back. To do that, I need help. You need to come to me if anyone does anything to hurt Phoebe again."

Abe nodded. "Alright. I'll do that."

"Good." Eric gestured to the cabin. "Mind if I talk to her?"

"Go ahead."

As Eric headed for the house, Abe watched him, surprised Eric placed value on people, especially people like him. He couldn't recall ever hearing any white person talking that way. And he did more than talk about justice. He actually put his words into action.

The door opened, and Phoebe's mother invited Eric in. The door shut, leaving Abe to wonder how Phoebe would respond now that Eric had done something about the situation. Abe hadn't been able to solve things to her satisfaction. Maybe she'd be happy with Eric's results.

Either way, it didn't matter. Abe would be putting her on the next stagecoach, and she'd be heading back to Ohio soon enough. Retrieving his pitchfork, he returned to the animals.

"PHOEBE, REMEMBER THAT nice young man who brought us here?" Phoebe's mother called out from the other side of the bedroom door.

Phoebe rolled over in the bed and called out, "Eric Johnson?"

"That's the one. He came here to talk to you."

Phoebe debated telling her mother to send him away. The last thing she felt like doing was talking to anyone. But then she thought about all the things Abe had told her about how things were for him. Perhaps Eric wanted to hear her side of the story, to find out whether or not Abe had defended her. It was possible Enoch and Benny had crafted some story to hurt him. That being the case, someone had to stand up and tell the truth, even if she was now a tainted woman from her association with him.

Clearing her throat, she sat up. "Tell him I'll be right there."

"Will do, dear," her mother replied.

From the other side of the closed door, her mother was talking to Eric in low, soothing tones, allowing Phoebe time to make herself presentable. She took a moment to wash the tears from her face. She knew she'd been sheltered most of her life, but it hadn't occurred to her just how protected she'd been until she came here.

Once she could trust herself to be calm, she went to the door and opened it. Eric was sitting in a chair, a cup of coffee in hand.

"There's really not much that happens in town," Eric was telling her mother who sat across from him. "Usually, the worst thing I have to worry about is breaking up a brawl at the saloon."

"It's nice there's not a lot of danger to worry about," her mother replied. "We heard all sorts of stories while we were coming here."

"I'm sure you did. There are elements of the West that are undesirable, but if you have the right people in positions of influence, things work themselves out nicely."

"It's a good thing you're the sheriff then." She glanced over at Phoebe and gestured to her. "Did you want to speak to my daughter alone?"

"It depends on what makes your daughter more comfortable." Eric rose to his feet. "Phoebe?"

"My mother can stay," Phoebe decided. She had, after all, already told her mother what happened in town. And if anything, her mother would support her story. She sat on the couch and waited for Eric to sit back in the chair before she asked, "How can I help you, Eric?"

"I wanted you to know I found out what happened with Enoch," Eric began, "and I know Benny didn't do anything to stop it."

Surprised, she glanced at her mother then back at him. "So, you know Abe came to my aid?"

"Yes, I know."

His soft voice settled her nerves. "I was afraid you'd think Abe did something wrong."

"I know Abe, and I know he wouldn't do anything to hurt anyone unless they deserved it. When I heard what happened, I knew Enoch and Benny were in the wrong. I just came by to tell you they're in jail. I told Abe, in the future, he should bring this kind of thing to my attention. I realize how things used to be for him, but it won't be that way anymore. He'll get fair treatment from me."

After all the things she'd gone through that day, this was so unexpected she had trouble believing her ears. But when her mother let out a cheer and thanked Eric, Phoebe realized she'd heard right.

"If Abe doesn't come to me, you can," Eric told Phoebe. "Either way, I'll do right by all of you."

"Thank you," Phoebe said. Then, after a moment of considering her words, she added, "Is it true that the people in town treat Abe poorly?"

"Yes, it is," Eric replied. "It's not something anyone talks about, but he doesn't get a fair shake. That's why I wanted to take care of things. Abe is reluctant to believe he has anyone to back him up. If you and I don't work together to make things better, things will stay as they've been. I can only do my part. I can't be everywhere at once. There's bound to be some things I'll miss. But change won't happen unless someone stands up to make things better."

Phoebe breathed a sigh of relief. Maybe being here wasn't going to be as awful as she'd feared. Maybe there was a chance to work things out, to live in contentment, to have the husband and children she'd always wanted. And it would be even better if she didn't have to make her mother go back to Ohio. Though her mother hadn't said anything, Phoebe could tell her mother liked the cabin and mountains. It was a quiet and beautiful area. And Phoebe liked it, too. So if she could do her part to make things better, she would.

"I understand," Phoebe told Eric. "Thank you for being a man of honor, Sheriff."

"I'm happy to do what I can." With a smile, Eric rose to his feet. "Next time you come into town, you can come and get me. I'll make sure no one harms you ever again."

Phoebe saw Eric to the door and closed it after he left. Then, unable to hide her curiosity, she looked out the window and watched as Abe left the barn to talk to him. Eric did most of the talking, only once gesturing to the cabin—probably because he was telling Abe what he'd told Phoebe. By the look on Abe's face, he didn't seem convinced the matter with Benny and Enoch was truly settled, but he nodded to Eric. Eric, in turn, got on his horse and left.

Abe's gaze went to Phoebe, and she almost turned from the window, embarrassed he'd caught her staring at him. But something in Abe's expression stopped her. She couldn't tell what it was, exactly. He had such a serious look on his face, and if she was right, he would do whatever it took to protect her.

Honestly, she wasn't sure what to make of it. There was nothing the least bit romantic about the silent exchange between them, but she felt a slight flutter in her stomach all the same. He really was a good looking man. Maybe there was a bit of darkness in his skin, but he still seemed more white than Indian. His hair was pulled back into a ponytail. Even so, she had the sudden inclination to touch it, to see if it was as soft as it appeared. He had a nice, solid build, too. Broad shoulders. Strong and tall, but not overpowering. And though the day's events had scared her, there was no denying he had protected her. He just might make a good husband after all.

He looked away from her, and she blinked, as if coming out of a daydream. Clearing her throat, she forced her attention to her mother, just now realizing she was saying something about what a nice sheriff they had in town.

"The world needs more people like him," her mother said as she headed for the kitchen. "Do you want something to drink?"

"Maybe some water," Phoebe replied, almost absentmindedly.

"I'll bring it right out. Why don't you sit down?"

With a nod, Phoebe went to the chair and settled into it, wondering how things might proceed from here.

Chapter Nine

Abe came in later than usual that evening. He'd purposely delayed doing the chores, mostly because he wasn't sure how to act around Phoebe or her mother after the day's events. After Eric talked to them, he figured it'd help put their minds at ease, but the fact remained, if Eric hadn't taken the move to put Enoch and Benny in jail, nothing would have been done.

Abe stared out the doorway of the barn, wondering if he should stay out here tonight. Who knew if someone would feel the need to retaliate because Eric chose to stand up for a half-breed?

The night would be the easiest time for someone to make their attack. If Abe was in the house, he might not hear the items he'd set out to jingle if they crossed the property line. He tapped his foot on the barn floor, giving a careful scan of the trees. There were far too many places a man could hide. But he'd been careful to make the string high enough to make them trip. If he stayed out here, would it frighten the women? Or would they feel safer?

With a heavy sigh, Abe rubbed his eyes. When he was alone, he didn't have this kind of pressure to deal with. If someone hurt him or his animals, no one else suffered for it. But now, someone could come after Phoebe or her mother. Too bad Eric had already promised himself to his mail-order bride. No one would dare harm Phoebe if she was meant for Eric.

He opened his eyes, this time his gaze going to the cabin. The front door opened, and he saw Phoebe step onto the porch. She glanced around until their eyes met. To his surprise, she closed the door behind her and headed toward him.

He made another scan of the area. He didn't think anyone was lurking out there. At least, he didn't see anyone. But just because he didn't see anyone, it didn't mean there wasn't someone there. It was on the tip of his tongue to warn her to go back to the cabin, but she ran over to him before he could get the words out.

"Is something wrong?" she asked, keeping her voice low as she reached him.

"Yes, there's something wrong. You're not in the cabin," he said.

"I came out to see if you're alright. We worried about you when you didn't come in after the chores were done."

She rubbed her arms and gave a slight shiver. Not only had she come out in the dark, but she hadn't even brought something to keep her warm. "I saw you standing in the doorway and thought there might be something I could do to help."

"I was just standing here," he shrugged, "and thinking."

"About what?"

After the day they'd shared, she had to ask him that? He noticed her shiver again, so he started unbuttoning his shirt.

"What are you doing?" she asked.

Noting the uncertainty in her tone, he said, "I'm only giving you my shirt so you can put it on." When she furrowed her eyebrows, he added, "To warm you up."

"Oh." In the light of the lantern, which hung on a hook nearby, he thought he detected a slight pink in her cheeks. "Thank you."

He slipped the shirt off and handed it to her, leaving on his undershirt. "I wasn't going to take off everything." Unable to refrain from the joke, he inserted, "I wasn't going to scare you."

She laughed as she put the shirt on. "I wouldn't be scared if you took everything off." Her eyes grew wide, and she gasped. "I don't mean

I expect you to take your clothes off. I-I...I, um, I know you weren't going to do it. Take everything off, I mean."

His lips curled up into a smile. She was rather adorable when she was stammering. "Don't worry. I know what you meant."

Relaxing, she chuckled, and the mood between them grew lighter.

"Look," he began, giving the area another good look, "I want to make sure you and your mother are safe. You should go back in."

"Why? Eric said Enoch and Benny are in jail."

How much should he tell her? He didn't want to frighten her, but it wasn't wise for her to be out in the open where anyone could find her.

"I'm going to sleep out here tonight," he finally said. "You and your mother don't have to worry about me."

"Where are you going to sleep?"

"Up there." He gestured to the loft. "I have everything I need in the trunk. You don't have to worry about me. Go on in and get some sleep. It's been a long day."

She glanced back at the cabin. "I'm not tired. I'd like to talk to someone."

"You can talk to your mother."

"She's already asleep. Can I stay out here for a while and talk to you?"

He glanced around the property again, and not sensing any danger, he nodded. "Alright, but we can't stay out here." He waved her into the barn.

She took a step in and paused. Just as he was about to ask if she'd changed her mind, she chuckled again. "I forgot how potent the smell is in here."

"Is it?" He saw the two cows and two horses. "I'm so used to it I don't even notice it anymore. But you're right. It smells like a..." The joke his uncle had often told him fell short of completion.

"It smells like what?" she asked, her expression indicating she wanted him to finish the joke.

"Nothing." There was no way he was going to say it smelled like a white man. While it was funny to him and his uncle, he doubted she'd find humor in it. "You want to sit?"

"Sure." She studied the area. "Where do you sit when you're in here?"

"When I'm not milking the cow," he glanced at the stool he used, "I sit over at that table. But there's only one chair, and the table isn't sturdy enough to hold you, even if you don't weigh much. I think the best place would be in the loft." He gestured to the ladder that would take them up to it. "I'm not sure you want to go there, though."

"Why not?"

He studied her expression, and sure enough, she was as naïve as the question was, which was surprising considering what she'd just been through in town earlier that day. But maybe it was a compliment. Maybe, just maybe, the question really meant she trusted him, that she knew he'd never hurt her. And that being the case, it was the nicest thing a white woman had ever done for him.

"Alright," he finally said. "I'll go first."

"I thought women usually went first and men followed," she replied as he went to the ladder.

"If I followed you, it'd give me a good view up your dress," he said.

"Oh, I hadn't thought of that."

"I know. But I did, and that's why I'm going up first."

He climbed the ladder and hurried to get out a blanket and pillow from his trunk. By the time she reached the top, he held his hand out to help her up.

Once she was sitting next to him, she asked, "How can you sleep here? It's not very comfortable."

"You get used to it," he replied. "Besides, I got more blankets in the trunk."

She nodded and wrapped his shirt more comfortably around her shoulders.

There was no denying it was cooler. Even he felt the slight chill. He retrieved one of the blankets. "Would you mind sharing this with me?"

"No."

He brought it around both of them, realizing too late this meant they would be touching each other. This wasn't exactly the image he had in mind when he suggested the blanket. It was on the tip of his tongue to apologize, but then she leaned against him, resting her head on his shoulder.

"Thank you," she said, her voice soft.

"It's just a blanket," he replied. "I've had it for years."

"No, that's not why I'm thanking you. With everything that happened today, I forgot to thank you for saving me from Enoch. I might not know much about what happens with a man and woman, but I know whatever he had in mind, it was going to hurt."

"I don't think it's supposed to hurt if the woman wants it."

At least, his mother never seemed to mind it when his father paid her visits. Even though he was as untried as Phoebe in the bedroom, it didn't take much of an imagination to know when the woman wanted it, it was something she enjoyed. He let out a long sigh. He didn't want to think about that. All his father had done was use her. Quite frankly, all the enjoyment she got out of it was quickly driven out by the tears she'd cry when he was gone.

"Enoch is a sorry excuse for a man," Abe said, pushing the past from his mind. "If I'd known Benny wasn't going to protect you, I wouldn't have left you alone. I thought Benny was one of the few who could be trusted." He shook his head. "Even knowing everything I do, I can be gullible."

"But you still came and stopped things before they went too far," she replied. "I was too hard on you. You did everything you knew to do. The way Benny talked about you and talked about me, I came to understand why you see things the way you do."

He stiffened. Benny talking about him was one thing, but him talking about her was another. "How did Benny talk about you?"

"I thought you'd be more curious about what he said about you than me. But since you asked, Benny said I was a distraction. He seems to think Carl brought me here so you'd stop the dispute over the land with the stream on it."

Benny was probably right. Carl would do anything to get him to stop claiming what was rightfully his. "Carl wants that property because he's convinced there's gold there."

"Is there?"

"No. Well, if there is, it's not much. I want that stream because I could use the water. White men worry about money too much. They'll force everyone off the land if they think there's a hint of gold or silver on it." In a lower voice, he added, "My people have been forced off their land for it."

"I never would have come out here if I'd known Carl was using me like that."

"I know. Carl used you for his gain. Just as his father used my mother for his," he grimaced, "pleasure. And that's how I became a bastard." Whether it was money or lust, it made little difference. "I'm sorry about what happened with Enoch and Benny today. I didn't realize Eric would have listened to me. Until the stagecoach arrives and I can get you and your mother safely on it so you can go back home, I won't let anyone harm you."

"I know you won't," she said. "I don't want to go back. Mother doesn't either. We want to stay here."

"After what happened today?"

"Yes. I had time to think about it, and I can't think of anyone else who'd be better for me and Mother than you." When he shook his head, she added, "Abe, you stood up to those men in town today, even though you thought it'd mean your life. You think I don't know why you set out that string and pots around the property? I bet you're sleep-

ing out here because you want to make sure if anyone does come, you'll
be ready for them. But more than that, you took us in when we needed
a safe place to stay, and you've been a gentleman the whole time. I know
I'm safe up here with you in this loft, too. I have a lot to learn about
the world, but one thing I know is when someone honorable and kind
comes along, that's the person you want to be with."

What was wrong with her? Did she really want this kind of life?
Not only did she give up the conveniences she'd no doubt been used
to in Ohio, but she'd been delegated to the same status as a half-breed.
Her lot in life would be much easier if she took a white husband.

Maybe it was the shock of the day's events talking. Maybe she
hadn't had sufficient time to process everything. Even he had been
prone to making foolish decisions when he hadn't given enough time
to consider all the possibilities before him. Yes. That had to be it. Give
her a couple of days, and she'd understand leaving was in her and her
mother's best interest.

Reassured by this logic, he didn't argue with her. He didn't know if
it was a trait all white women shared, but she seemed particularly stubborn. He'd often wished his mother hadn't been so eager to let his father have everything he'd wanted. It would have been better for all of
them, especially her, if she'd learned to stand her ground. But she never
had, and to this day, he blamed her death on her weakness.

"Are you sure you want to spend the whole night here?" Phoebe
asked, breaking him out of his thoughts. "It'd be warmer in the house."

"Yes, I'm sure," he replied. "I've spent nights out here when it was
chillier than this."

"Oh? When?"

"When I was growing up." It was better to be out here than in the
house when his father came to spend the night with his mother. Before
she could wiggle this information from him, he said, "I'll walk you back
to the cabin."

He made a move to get up, but she put her hand on his arm, stopping him. "Can I stay a little longer? It's peaceful out here."

"But I thought you were cold."

"It doesn't feel cold when I'm with you."

"Alright." He settled back to where he'd been sitting before. He couldn't blame her for wanting to linger out here. It was quiet. In many ways, it was soothing. "Let me know when you're ready to go back."

"I will."

She rested her head on his shoulder again and snuggled against him. "This is a lot different from where I grew up."

"I'm sure it is."

"There were people everywhere. Even at night, you could hear someone talking on the streets beneath your apartment window. I didn't know a place could be this quiet."

He didn't know how to respond to that, so he decided to remain silent. If she wanted to say more, she could. But as it turned out, she grew silent, too. At first, he didn't care much for the lack of conversation. As the minutes passed, however, he got used to it, and soon, he was thinking it was nice to be able to share a quiet moment with someone else where neither one felt the need to fill in the silence with idle chatter.

Relaxing, he let out a slow breath. It was a shame there weren't more moments like this in life. Too often, problems kept getting in the way, preventing him from receiving any enjoyment. He'd had to grow up fast, and he'd learned there was a lot of sorrow in the world. Pleasant moments, such as this, were rare. It was just like the times when his mother had held him and sang one of her songs when he was little. He closed his eyes and soaked in the experience.

The minutes passed, one easing into another, and he lost all sense of time. He couldn't recall a time when he felt more at peace. His mind wandered, not focusing on any one thing, except for maybe the sounds around him.

There was no sense of danger. The pots and pans he'd set up along the property remained untouched. That was good. The longer the night passed without incident, the better. The last thought that drifted through his mind was how warm he was despite sleeping out in the barn.

Chapter Ten

The next morning when Phoebe woke up, she was snuggled up against someone warm with a solid frame. At first, she thought it was a dream, but then she became aware of the man's chest rising and falling in a smooth and steady rhythm. Her eyes flew open, and she sat up.

Abe slept on his back, his eyes closed and his hair loosened from his ponytail. She wanted to touch it, to find out if it was as soft as it looked. She'd get away with it much easier while he was sleeping. But even as her fingers itched to do so, she held back. No, it was best not to do it without him knowing.

She looked at the barn entrance and saw it was just past dawn. Good. She might make it back to the cabin before her mother woke. This, of course, should have been her primary concern, not the whole matter of touching his hair. She had her reputation to protect, after all.

Without waking Abe, she wrapped the blanket around him. Then she climbed down the ladder and hurried out of the barn, ignoring the impatient neighing and mooing from the animals. Abe would soon feed them. She'd do it herself if he'd shown her what to do.

Oh, this was silly. She had more important matters to tend to. Her mother would be waking up soon. Repeating this to herself, she hurried through the process of relieving her bladder. By the time she made it to the cabin, it felt like an entire hour passed. Realistically, it was probably more like five minutes. But it was easy to lose the proper perspective of time when worried someone might catch her doing something improper.

Her heart was pounding in her chest as she opened the door and peered into the quiet cabin. Good. Her mother wasn't up yet. Breathing a sigh of relief, she went to the kitchen and got a pot of coffee started. She was ready to make oatmeal when she remembered Abe had taken the pots and pans out of the kitchen yesterday to set up his warning system.

With a frown, she considered her other options. Pancakes were out of the question, too, but there was some bread, cheese, and butter. It wouldn't be the best breakfast, but until she got her cooking supplies back, it'd have to do.

She had just cut three slices of bread when she heard her mother's familiar footsteps. Glancing over her shoulder, she smiled. "Morning, Ma. Did you sleep well?"

"I did, but I noticed you never made it to the bedroom," her mother replied, amusement in her voice.

Phoebe's face grew warm.

"You're also wearing Abe's shirt," her mother pointed out.

Gasping, Phoebe looked down at the shirt. "It's not what it looks like," she quickly told her mother, unsure if her anxious tone made things worse. "After you went to sleep, I got bored and went to see what Abe was doing. I was cold, so he let me borrow his shirt. We talked for a while, and then I fell asleep. I didn't mean to fall asleep. I didn't think I was that tired."

Her mother chuckled and held her hand up to stop her. "I know you wouldn't do anything unless you were married. Besides, you're not good at lying."

"I'm not?"

"No. You won't look me in the eyes if you're trying to pull a fast one on me. Now, what are you making for breakfast?"

Phoebe relaxed. "Just bread, cheese, and butter. Abe took the pots and pans. He only left this coffee pot." She gestured to it. "Coffee should be ready in a few minutes."

"He doesn't trust people easily."

"No, he doesn't. But after yesterday, I can't blame him. Some people really don't treat him with the same respect they'd give someone who was fully white."

"I wish I'd gone with you to town. There's power in numbers. I could have hit that Enoch and Benny for the way they treated you."

"Thankfully, Abe came just in time."

"Do you feel better this morning?"

Phoebe nodded. "I still don't like the idea of going to town, but yes, I feel better. Abe was there to protect me."

"I could tell he was angry about what happened. I don't think he'll leave you alone in town ever again."

"No, he probably won't."

Once again, she decided not to tell her mother he was planning to send them back to Ohio. For one, it wasn't going to happen. Despite what Abe thought, her mother didn't have another long and tedious journey in her. Two, there was nothing to go back to. And three, having spent time alone with him, she thought they'd do well together.

Maybe he didn't see it yet, but she did. Despite their shaky beginning, she saw a very promising future for them. She just hoped, in time, he would see it, too.

Phoebe removed the shirt, figuring it best. She didn't want Abe to come in for breakfast and worry her mother might be thinking something happened when it hadn't. After glancing around for a suitable place to put it, she finally settled on setting it in the laundry hamper.

"I know it's not something we would normally do at breakfast," her mother began when Phoebe returned to the kitchen, "but we can have some pie. Who says you can't have it first thing in the morning?"

Grinning at her mother's question, she said, "No one. And if anyone disagrees, we don't have to let them know we did it."

Satisfied, her mother hurried to get the pie.

ABE HAD NO IDEA WHEN Phoebe returned to the cabin. She might have been foolish enough to do it while it was still dark. When he saw she and her mother were setting the table, he relented in reminding her how dangerous it was to be outside by herself before the sun rose.

Phoebe glanced over at him and smiled, and something about the way she looked at him made him forget the admonition on his tongue.

"I hope you don't mind," Phoebe began, "but we're going to have bread with slices of cheese and butter for breakfast."

"And leftover pie for dessert," her mother added.

"Right," Phoebe said. "That, too. The only pot we could find was the coffee pot. Otherwise, we would have made something more fitting for breakfast."

"Oh, the pots and pans." Abe's eyes widened. "I didn't think to leave a couple here. I'm sorry. Those were the first things I thought of."

"No need to apologize," her mother said. "We know why you took them, and it was nice of you to protect us."

"We were just wondering if there's something else we can use in their place," Phoebe added. "Are there any tools or any other objects you have that will clang together like those pots and pans do?"

"I'd hate to use the tools," he replied. "I need them." Then, just so they understood he realized they were in a similar predicament, he amended, "Just as you need pots and pans." He shifted from one foot to another as he thought over all the possible things he might have, but his mind came up blank. He opened his mouth, ready to tell them this when he recalled Travis Martin, the town recluse. "Well, there is someone who might have something I can use. He has a lot of junk no one has any use for."

"He collects junk on purpose?" Phoebe asked.

Amused at the shocked tone in her voice, he grinned. "He takes old things and creates new things from them. He's actually good at it."

Her mother waved him over to the table. "Do you have anything he made?"

Obeying her silent invitation to the table, he sat in one of the chairs but waited for them to sit before he answered. "Actually, he fixed up a wagon and sold it to me for cheap. I also got a good trunk in the barn and that worktable," he gestured to the table, "from him. He even sold me some of the tools I use and that coffee pot over there. He can make anything."

Her mother poured coffee into their cups. "Sounds like he has a gift."

He took the cup she handed him and thanked her before taking a sip. Every time he drank it, it reminded him of the white men who drank it so much, but, since Phoebe and her mother seemed to like it, he supposed it wasn't so bad. Besides, they had a way of making it that made it taste better than anything his mother did when she'd make it for his father. It was probably the bitter connection to his father that bothered him the most when it came to coffee. Now, at least, he'd have something pleasant to connect it with.

"I'll go see Travis today," he said as he spread some butter on his slice of bread. "You two will have to go along with me. I don't like the thought of you staying here alone."

He glanced at them to see if they would argue with him, but Phoebe smoothed the napkin on her lap and smiled. "Since you had nice things to say about Travis, we have no doubt he's a good man. It'll be nice to meet a good person while in town."

"Well, he doesn't live in town. He keeps out of the way, and I don't know if he'll let you actually meet him." When he noticed their frowns, he quickly added, "He's terribly shy, especially around women, and the prettier they are, the worse it gets for him." He motioned to them. "You two will intimidate him."

"Oh, Abe," her mother said with a laugh, "I wouldn't have taken you for a flirt." She waved her hand at him, her cheeks pink.

Not sure what she meant by "a flirt", he replied, "Granted, you're older. You're Phoebe's mother, after all, but it's easy to see where Phoebe got her good looks."

This time it was Phoebe who blushed.

For the life of him, he couldn't figure out why they should react this way. He glanced at one and then the other. "I only speak the truth. Don't any of the white men remark on your beauty?"

"Not in such a pleasant way," her mother replied.

Her mother gave Phoebe a look that implied something, but he couldn't be sure what it was. All he knew was that they were happy with him. He supposed that was good enough. He turned his attention back to buttering the bread, deciding to put their secret look aside. Who knew what women were thinking?

The important thing was, they'd all go to Travis' together, and with any luck, the trip would be uneventful and boring. After everything that happened yesterday, he'd welcome uneventful and boring.

Chapter Eleven

Phoebe couldn't stop the butterflies in her stomach as Abe led the wagon through the small town. Though she sat between Abe and her mother, she couldn't help feeling vulnerable, especially when they passed the general store. She caught sight of a movement from within and saw that a different man was managing the place in Benny's absence.

Maybe that should have made her feel better. It meant Benny and Enoch were still in jail. But it didn't make her feel better. It only reminded her of how quickly she'd gone from feeling safe to realizing she'd been in danger.

More than that, she caught sight of a woman, who made it a point to tell her young son not to make eye contact with "that sort" before she picked him up and hurried away from them.

Phoebe frowned. Just what did the woman think she, her mother, and Abe were going to do to them?

Her gaze went from the woman to a couple of men on the other side of the street. One nudged his friend in the side and nodded in Abe's direction. The other shook his head, and she read his lips as he told his friend, "Half breed and his whore."

Whore? She thought Eric had taken her and her mother to Abe to protect them so she wouldn't get that kind of reputation. Was that why Enoch felt he had every right to treat her the way he did? Was it why Benny didn't do anything about it? They really and truly saw her as no better than a prostitute at the saloon?

She didn't notice she was squeezing both Abe's and her mother's arms until Abe whispered, "Focus on the path in front of you. Don't let any of them know they can upset you. If you let them know they can bother you, you give them power."

Clasping her hands in her lap, she directed her gaze forward. This technique of ignoring people wasn't an easy one. Her mother had raised her to be polite, always smiling and greeting those they passed by, but in this town, the rules were different.

As they passed one of the houses, she noticed her mother waving to someone and turned her attention to an elderly woman sitting on her front porch. The woman was smiling and waving. Surprised, Phoebe followed her mother's lead and returned the gesture. At least there was one kind person in town besides Eric.

In short time, Abe led the wagon out of town and up a winding path lined with trees. The path had several sharp turns in it. Phoebe had to hold onto Abe's arm in order to avoid bumping into her mother. If she hadn't done so, her poor mother would have ended up falling off the wagon.

"I think Travis made the road up to his house this way to dissuade anyone from coming here," he told Phoebe and her mother.

It was on the tip of Phoebe's tongue to ask him if he wished he'd thought to do the same thing to his property, but then thought better of it. From the sound of it, he hadn't had any control over that.

When the path came to an end, there was a small cottage tucked among a group of trees. In a larger area was a large building, and next to that was a barn. Weeds and vines had popped up along both the building and the barn. Paint was chipping on the barn and building, and it looked like there were some repairs needed on them. For all she knew, the same was true for the cottage. It was just too hard to tell with all the trees in the way. Had it not been for the garden by the cottage and the few animals surrounding the barn, she would have believed the place had been abandoned.

Abe set the brake and turned to her and her mother. "I'll be back. You better wait here. If he sees you two, he'll probably take off running and hide."

"Women really do intimidate him?" Phoebe asked, still unable to believe it.

"They do when they're pretty."

He said it so matter-of-factly, he couldn't have realized he was paying them a compliment. He just hopped off the wagon and went to the large building as if he'd said nothing out of the ordinary.

"That's the second time he's called you pretty," her mother whispered.

Heat rose up into her face. "He included you in that comment."

"Yes, and I know he meant it, but it has a special meaning for you. You're the one he's going to marry."

Phoebe's gaze went to Abe as he knocked on the door to the building. "I don't know, Ma," she softly said.

"You're not sure you want to marry him?" her mother asked.

"No, it's not that," she replied, choosing her words carefully. "It's...well...I'm not sure he's convinced it's safe for us to be here. You know, after what happened yesterday."

"No one can blame him for worrying. I can tell he feels like it was partly his fault since he left you in the general store alone."

"It shouldn't have made any difference if he'd been there or not. That should never have happened. It wasn't like I went into the saloon."

"I know." Her mother patted her hand in the familiar, comforting gesture she'd used when Phoebe was little. "Neither one of you did anything wrong."

The door to the building opened, and though Phoebe caught a glimpse of Travis, she couldn't get a good look at him. He was taller and wider than Abe. He looked like a tower of a man. Not fat, but definitely husky. As for his face, she couldn't tell what he looked like since he wore a hat and looked down at Abe.

She saw him shift to the side, further hiding himself from her view. Abe glanced back at her and her mother before turning back to him. She wasn't sure, but she suspected Travis intentionally shifted away so she and her mother couldn't see him.

"The preacher's due out soon," Phoebe said, turning her attention back to her mother. "What if Abe's still worried? I don't have much time to reassure him everything will be alright if he marries me." And she couldn't guarantee it to herself, either. It was only by faith she was willing to make the leap.

"What is your alternative?" her mother asked.

"The stagecoach comes again in three weeks." She couldn't bring herself to voice the rest.

"Is that what you want to do? Because, Phoebe," her mother patted her hand again, "if you want to go back to Ohio, you know I'll agree to it. I don't want you to be unhappy."

"I like him. I admit, at first, he scared me somewhat. I thought there was no way I could ever be comfortable with him."

Her mother's eyes grew wide. "When did this happen?"

"While I was helping him with the roof." Before her mother could ask for details, she said, "He's half-Indian and half-white. He's got a lot of bitterness about the wrongs done to him. I can't blame him. Not after what happened in town. People don't think too well of me because I'm with him. Their opinion of him seems to have become their opinion of me."

"That can be a difficult thing to overcome." After a long pause, her mother said, "Phoebe, don't stay here because of me. I'm willing to go back to Ohio."

She had no doubt her mother would be willing to make the trip, but she didn't know if her mother was strong enough to handle it. It had taken a lot out of both of them. She glanced at Abe again. He was a strong man. He was a good man. He was the kind of man who would defend those he loved to the point of sacrifice. She'd be hard pressed to find anyone better. And more than that, she did have a growing attraction for him.

"I want to marry him," Phoebe said. "I think I could love him."

"Then treat him as you would treat a white man. Let him know you consider him to be your equal."

"I already do. When I look at him, I don't see someone who's a half-breed. I see Abe Thomas."

"Then I expect the rest will fall into place as you two get to know each other better."

Phoebe nodded, hoping her mother was right.

"YOU DON'T NEED TO PAY me for the metal scraps," Travis told Abe. "They're worthless junk. I can't do anything with them."

"I want to," Abe said. "It's important I pay for what I get."

"I understand. Well, let me think."

As Travis thought over a fair amount, he lifted his hat and ran his hand through his dark blonde hair, something that must have been an unconscious habit since he immediately put the hat back on his head. His face turned red, and he hurried over to the pile of discarded metal pieces in the corner of the building.

It was on the tip of Abe's tongue to tell him he wasn't as ugly as he believed himself to be, but he kept his mouth closed. He didn't need to tell a grown man what to think. People in town talked way too much, and they'd made Travis seem more like a monster than an actual man.

So what if he had some scars on his face and body from a childhood bout of varicella? He couldn't help that any more than he could help the fact that he was six-foot-five with a heavy build. Some things were out of his control, just as Abe had had no choice in who his father was. But both were still cast aside. Of all the white men Abe had dealt with, he figured only Travis could really understand him.

"How many scraps do you need?" Travis called out.

"You got thirty?" Abe asked.

"I do."

"How much for them?"

Travis set his hands on his hips. "How does twenty cents sound?"

Abe shook his head. "You've got to be the only white man who sells things at a price lower than they're worth. Fifty cents."

"They're junk, Abe."

"Not for what I need them for."

"Fine. Fifty cents. Want to come over? You can pick the sizes you want, and we'll load them up in the wheelbarrow."

Abe went over to help him, careful not to nick himself as he placed the scraps in a pile. He picked the larger pieces, thinking the lower the pitch they'd produce when struck together, the easier it'd be to hear them.

When the wheelbarrow was full, Travis said, "Take them out to your wagon. I'll continue gathering the largest pieces I can find while you're gone."

"Alright."

Abe took the wheelbarrow out to the wagon, not the least bit surprised when Phoebe asked, "Where's Travis?"

"Gathering more pieces for me," he replied as he started putting the metal into the back of the wagon. Before she could ask anything else, he added, "I told you he doesn't want to show himself to ladies, especially pretty ones. If you were covered in warts and had three arms instead of two, he might venture out here. But since that's not the case, he's staying put."

He finished unloading the wheelbarrow and went back to the building.

As promised, Travis had collected the rest of the scraps. "I have twenty more pieces if you want to take more with you. No extra charge," he added.

"I think thirty will be enough, but if I need more, I'll be back."

It wasn't until they were halfway into filling up the wheelbarrow that Abe noticed Travis' gaze going to the window where there was a good view of the wagon.

With a chuckle, Abe asked, "Didn't you hear about Carl posting that mail-order bride ad on my behalf?"

Travis almost dropped the scrap he was holding. "Carl did what?"

"I thought everyone knew."

"Well, no one told me about it." He shrugged. "Not that I would have believed it if they had. I would have thought even someone like Carl would have better sense than to mess with you. You can be a force to be reckoned with. Word is you came within an inch of setting his no good behind on fire when he tried to get your cabin."

Despite the grim reminder that Carl had tried to kick him off his property, Abe chuckled. "I barely missed with that flaming arrow. All people like him know how to do is take."

Abe thought back to the dispute over the stream lining his proper-ty. Carl only wanted it because he thought there might be gold there. He had no concern over the value of the water in itself, nor did he care Abe had to either dig a new well or dig his current one deeper when he ran out of water. All the while, Carl had a good well that never went dry.

With a sigh, Abe let his gaze go to Phoebe, who was talking to her mother. Did Carl honestly believe if he had a wife, he'd give up on the stream? Didn't it ever occur to him that having a wife was an even greater reason to have a reliable water source?

"I know your uncle had set up lodging for you and your mother by that stream before your father came along and found it," Travis said.

Abe thought he detected a hint of compassion in Travis' voice, but when he looked back at Travis, Travis was putting more scraps in the wheelbarrow, so it was hard to know if he'd been imagining it.

Abe picked up the rest of the large pieces and said, "I'll get it back. It's just a matter of how I'm going to do it."

Travis nodded. Whether he was nodding to indicate he wished Abe luck or if he believed Abe would do it, it didn't matter. At least he was showing support, something most people wouldn't do. And for that, Abe appreciated having Travis in the town. He and Eric were probably the only two redeeming qualities of the place.

Once the wheelbarrow was full, Abe took it out to the wagon. After he loaded it with the rest of the metal pieces, he returned to Travis and paid him.

The ride back to his place was as quiet as it'd been on the way to Travis'. He tried not to dwell too much on the fact that Phoebe struggled with keeping her gaze forward. Despite his suggestion, he noticed she'd glance around them from time to time. Worse, she stiffened a couple of times, which made him also look at the townsfolk, though he kept willing himself not to give into that temptation. It was bad enough to know the people either warned their children to stay away from them or shook their heads in disapproval. He didn't need to see it.

What made Phoebe think she could be content living here for the rest of her life? This would be her experience every time she went to town if she persisted in giving them power over her. Did she really want to deal with this all the time?

His mother had been too soft for the kind of life she'd been given. And now he had another soft female to contend with. At least Phoebe's mother wasn't disturbed by any of it. Or, if she was, she was doing a good job of hiding it.

Abe relaxed as he guided his horses up the path that would take him home. One way or another, he was going to see to it that Phoebe and her mother went on the stagecoach when it came into town. She deserved better than this, and he'd make sure she got it.

Chapter Twelve

For the next few days, Phoebe decided to pretty up the cabin. If she was going to make a home for her and her mother here, it was time she added her special touch to the place. And in all honesty, it was fun to think of how she could transform the cabin from a bachelor's home to that of a married man.

Since she'd already taken the time to sweep the floors, clean the windows, and dust the furniture, she could devote her attention to helping her mother with the curtains. The two spent considerable time on the porch, enjoying the warm weather and sunlight while they worked. From time to time, they talked about Phillip and his family, and in doing so, they took a break from their work to write them a missive to let them know everything that had happened.

"Next time we're in town, we'll send it off," her mother said after Phoebe finished writing her portion of it.

From there, they returned to their work and made guesses on whether Phillip's next child would be a girl or a boy, each knowing they probably wouldn't find out for a few months, given how long it took to send or receive anything all the way out here.

When they finished with the curtains, they placed them throughout the cabin, and as they finished with Abe's room, Phoebe took a moment to give the room a good inspection. Up to now, she hadn't given serious consideration to the fact that this would also be her room once they married.

Butterflies fluttered around in her stomach. Just how would things change between them once the preacher joined them as husband and wife? At the moment, they had settled into a quiet routine, and they seemed to be getting along fine. Most of her time was still spent with her mother, but she suspected that would change once she started sleeping in here.

"You don't like the way the room looks?" her mother asked, breaking her out of her thoughts.

"No, it's not that," Phoebe replied.

The room was quaint in its appearance. Though it belonged to a bachelor, Abe had chosen to leave a couple of things his mother must have made for him. There was a quilt best suited for a child neatly folded on the chair in the corner of the room. A set of blocks and a wooden horse were neatly set on top of it. Other than that, the simple dresser and bed were about all the furnishings in the room.

Phoebe thought the brown curtains gave the room a more rustic feel. They were a little frilly on the ends, which made them more feminine, but she thought Abe would prefer the darker color. So really, they were a blend of her and Abe, something she hoped he wouldn't mind. She hadn't thought to seek his advice before starting the project, and honestly, it wasn't until this moment she regretted this error in judgment. She shouldn't have assumed he'd be happy with the changes she was making.

She turned to her mother. "Do you think he'll like what we're doing with this cabin?"

"I don't know if men concern themselves with how a home looks," her mother replied. "Your pa never seemed to notice anything I did, and Phillip didn't seem to care when Beatrice put up pink, lacy curtains. I think men expect women to decorate the home however they see fit, but if you're worried, you should ask Abe. Then you can set your mind at ease."

Phoebe knew her mother was right, but she wasn't looking forward to that particular conversation. He'd been pretty determined to see her and her mother on the next stagecoach the last time they'd been in town. She didn't know if the past few days had changed his mind or not.

"You're right," Phoebe said, scanning the room again. "I should talk to him." Taking a deep breath, she faced her mother. "Wish me luck?"

Her mother gave her an understanding smile then hugged her. "You've always been so hesitant, but in the end, you get things done. I have no doubt you'll find a way to convince him the cabin is much better with your personal touch."

"You helped."

"Yes, but this is your home. No matter what people say, the wife is the one the house truly belongs to."

"Is that why Pa always said the best thing he could do for you was to stay out of your way?" Phoebe asked, unable to resist teasing her mother.

Her mother chuckled. "That's exactly why he said that. He was a smart man, and Abe is smart, too. I'm sure all your fears are for nothing. You'll feel better after you talk to him."

She hoped her mother was right. So far, nothing had turned out like she'd hoped when she answered the mail-order bride ad. But Abe had been good. He hadn't once taken advantage of her, and he had the perfect opportunity the night she'd accidently fallen asleep in the barn loft with him. He'd set up the metal scraps around the property and helped them wash the pots and pans when he'd brought them back to the kitchen. He'd brought her and her mother food from the garden. He'd hunted and skinned three small animals so she and her mother were spared having to cut up the meat. She honestly didn't know how he managed to stomach it. The sight alone had made her queasy when she stumbled upon him skinning the rabbits he'd caught.

Life was drastically different out here than it'd been in Ohio, but it was lovely in the evenings. One of her favorite pastimes was sitting on the porch and listening to the birds sing. From time to time, she'd venture up on the barn roof to get a good look at the mountains.

There was a beauty to being surrounded by a lot of trees, and in many ways, the rest of the world seemed to fade away. The hustle and bustle of the city was long gone, and surprisingly, she didn't miss all the places she'd gone shopping. How quickly she'd gotten used to a new environment.

With one last glance at her mother, she smiled then headed outside. She didn't find Abe right away. He wasn't in the barn or in the garden. When she did find him, she saw him bending over one of his traps. Upon closer inspection, she saw he was prying the trap open, so he could release the dead coyote from it. A bloody knife was beside Abe, and the ground beneath the body was red.

Abe glanced over his shoulder, and when his eyes met hers, he shook his head. "I think I destroyed the fur. I try to be careful if I have to kill an animal I trap."

"You keep the fur when you skin animals?"

He nodded and gathered the coyote in his arms. "I look for things to make with it. Usually, I make blankets or rugs, but from time to time, I line clothes to make them warmer. The rug in front of the fireplace came from three animals. I try not to let anything from the animal go to waste. It's something my uncle taught me."

"That's a good idea." She stepped aside so he could get around her. As she followed him, she asked, "My mother and I thought it might be nice to pretty up the cabin. You noticed us sewing on the porch the last few days, didn't you?"

"I thought you were working on a dress."

"No, we were working on curtains."

"Curtains? Why were you doing those?"

She shrugged. "I thought the windows looked bare." She followed him into the barn. "Do you want me to help you with anything?"

"Would you get a blanket out from that trunk over there," he gestured to the corner of the barn, "and roll it out on that table?" He nodded toward the small table under a window.

She hurried to obey and watched as he set the dead animal gently on the blanket.

"I don't usually catch an animal this big," he told her. "He has such a beautiful coat." He shook his head. "I shouldn't have been so careless when I cut his throat."

"You didn't mean to be careless."

"It doesn't matter whether I meant to be careless or not. The fact is, I was." He lifted the lid from the trunk and picked up an empty pail. "I'll see how bad the damage is after I clean it. Maybe something can be saved."

She stepped in front of him before he could leave the barn. "Abe, I wish you wouldn't be so hard on yourself."

"I've been trapping coyotes and other animals since I was seven. There's no excuse for such carelessness."

"But these things happen. We all have our moments."

"When you need to preserve the fur, you can't afford those kind of moments." He let out a heavy sigh. "It doesn't matter. I can't go back and undo the damage. I'll save what I can and do better next time."

She bit her lower lip, so she wouldn't remind him this wasn't the end of the world. Abe was surprisingly hard on himself when he didn't perform a task up to his standards. She'd never come across someone who demanded perfection of himself before. Just what was she supposed to say to him?

Maybe she wasn't supposed to say anything. Maybe she was better off leaving him alone. Abe seemed like the kind of man who'd rather be alone when he was upset.

She returned to the house, and her mother asked, "What did he say about the curtains?"

It was then Phoebe remembered why she'd gone out there to talk to him. She debated going back out, but considering what happened with the coyote, she thought better of it. Since her mother was still looking at her expectantly, Phoebe said, "I don't know. We'll just have to take our chances that the curtains are alright. He caught a coyote, and he's too busy to talk."

Her mother nodded. "Let's hang up the other curtains in our bedroom."

Glad her mother didn't press the issue, she gathered the light green curtains and followed her mother to the bedroom.

IT WASN'T UNTIL ABE settled in his bed for the night that he noticed the curtains. Eyebrows furrowed, he studied them, noting the way they blocked the moonlight from streaming in through the window. Since when did he have curtains? He was sure he hadn't had them last night.

Then he remembered his conversation with Phoebe earlier that day when she found him at the trap. She'd mentioned something about curtains. But she'd chosen to put curtains in his room, and this signified something important. He was sure of it. A woman didn't put curtains in a man's room unless she was planning to make this her room, too.

His gut tightened. She had no intention of leaving. Even after going into town and seeing firsthand how little people thought of her because of her association with him, she planned to marry him. He didn't understand her at all. What kind of woman wanted this kind of life? Did she really enjoy knowing there were scraps of metal around the cabin and barn? Did she honestly think once Benny and Enoch were out of jail, things would be as quiet as they were now?

Yes, she probably did. She probably assumed because Eric Johnson put them in jail, that was the end of it. But it wasn't. Enoch might go to the saloon and end up too drunk to care, but Benny wasn't so forgiving. Abe should have known better than to believe Benny wouldn't let any harm come to Phoebe because she was white. He should have realized his association with Phoebe would make Benny think less of her. Well, that was an error in judgment he wouldn't make again.

If she'd get on the stagecoach when it came, it'd make things so much easier. But those curtains told him what he feared most. Soon, it wouldn't just be him he'd have to defend. There would be two women he'd be responsible for. His uncle had thought he could protect him and his mother, and he'd paid for that mistake with his life.

Just the reminder brought an image of Gene Carter's sneer to mind. He'd put the rifle over his shoulder right after killing his uncle and turned to Abe, who'd been ten at the time. "Let that be a lesson to you, half-breed. You don't give us what we want, and you'll pay for it." Then he'd gone into the cabin and forced himself upon Abe's mother.

Gritting his teeth, Abe stared at the ceiling, once again wishing he knew where Gene lived. But the man lived like a vagabond, only popping up in town once in a while, and it seemed Abe missed him each time. There was a day of reckoning. Abe could feel it in his gut. He'd known it since that night he was ten. Somehow, someway, he knew there was a day coming when the tables would be turned, and he'd be the one pointing the rifle at Gene.

Sometimes, it was the only thing that got him through the day. He owed it to his uncle and his mother. He owed it to every Cherokee who'd suffered at the hand of the white men because they thought the Cherokee were beneath them.

Abe's gaze went back to the curtains. Curse it! He didn't like this. If he was honest with himself, he had to admit he liked having those curtains there. But if Phoebe and her mother stayed, it left him vulnerable, and he didn't like being vulnerable.

He hated Carl Richie for putting him in this position. Carl knew exactly what he was doing. Carl had been hoping for this, had hoped Abe would like having her around. But Abe couldn't give in. Giving in would be the worst thing he could do. He had to remember what happened to his uncle and his mother. It hadn't ended well for either of them. He had to stay strong. He couldn't allow himself to be vulnerable. Ever.

Chapter Thirteen

"We're going to town?" Phoebe asked Abe the next morning as everyone was having breakfast.

"I need to take care of something, and I can't leave you two here," Abe replied, glancing between Phoebe and her mother. "I'll leave you with Eric. You'll be in good hands."

She glanced at the eggs on her fork before directing her gaze back to him. "What do you need to take care of?"

He'd expected her to ask that question, which was why he already had an answer. "I'm going to have a talk with Carl."

She dropped her fork on the plate. Jerking, she hurried to gather the portion of eggs that had landed on the table. Once it was back on her plate, she turned to him. "Why are you going to see Carl?"

"Because I have a point to make." When her eyebrows furrowed and she opened her mouth to ask him another question, he quickly added, "He needs to know I'm not going to give up on that stream and twenty acres. My uncle was here before Carl's family came to this land. Carl brought you out here in hopes I'd let it go, but I'm not. I'm going to keep fighting for it."

He almost didn't tell them the last part, but he figured they had a right to know what had prompted Carl to bring them out here.

He wiped his mouth with the cloth napkin and set it on his plate. "Thank you for the wonderful meal. I'm going to finish my chores. Then I'll bring the wagon over here. We'll leave in about an hour."

He stood up, fully expecting that to be the end of the discussion, but Phoebe followed him as he left the house. "Is that what Benny meant when he said I was a distraction?"

Surprised by the question, he stopped as he went down the last step of the porch and turned in her direction. She closed the distance between them until she was in front of him, an expectant look on her face.

"When I went to the general store, Benny said Carl brought me here to be a distraction," she continued. "Is this about the stream and land?"

As much as Abe hated to be so blunt, he didn't see what good hiding the truth would be. And who knew? Maybe she had to know. Maybe it'd speak some sense into her so she wouldn't waste the rest of her life with him.

"Yes, you are supposed to be a distraction," he said. "Carl brought you out here for his own benefit. He wasn't thinking of what was best for you. He was thinking of what was best for him. And what's best for him is if he keeps his claim to that property." He pointed toward it. "That's what men like Carl do. They take what they want, and when someone fights to keep it, they set up obstacles to prevent him from keeping it."

Her cheeks grew red, and he could tell by the look in her eyes that this news hurt her. But what was he supposed to do? Lie and tell her Carl's motives were good? Men like Carl weren't good. The worst mistake anyone could make was in trusting his kind.

"Phoebe," he began, his voice taking on a gentler tone, "you belong where men don't use people as pawns. Your association with me isn't in your favor. You saw what happened with Enoch and Benny. And now you can see why Carl brought you here. This isn't the kind of place a good person belongs."

"You're here, and you're good."

"I didn't choose to be here. I was born here. My grandparents were forced off their farm in Georgia because of the gold. My uncle was thirteen at the time, and my mother had just been born. My uncle and mother had three other siblings, one brother and two sisters. My uncle was the oldest and my mother was the youngest.

"He told me about how the white men forced them off their land in 1838 and put them into camps while they waited to find out what to do with them. During this time, conditions were so bad only my grandfather, my uncle, and my mother survived. My grandfather's brother was one of the Cherokees who signed the treaty to remove us from our land. The Cherokees found out what his brother did and killed him for betraying his people.

"My grandfather feared for the safety of my uncle and mother because of their association with his brother and fled north. My grandfather got sick and died along the way. It was my uncle, who was only fourteen by then, who found this land and built a home for himself and my mother.

"I don't belong with the white man, and I don't belong with the Cherokee. This land is all I have, and I will fight to the death to keep it. That's what this whole thing is about. It's about Carl getting his hands on gold that might or might not be in the stream. People die for gold, Phoebe. I had aunts, an uncle, and grandparents I never knew because of it. Do you honestly think I want to lose you over it, too? You need to get on the stagecoach when it comes. It's your best chance of happiness in this life."

Phoebe didn't seem like she knew how to respond to that, and he couldn't blame her. He'd just given her so much information there was no way she could adequately process it all at once. She needed time to think over it. And he was sure once she did, she would understand leaving was the best course for her to take.

"I'll see to it you and your mother return to Ohio," he said. "Then the next time you answer a mail-order bride ad, make sure you're going to a place big enough where if this happens again, you have plenty of bachelors to choose from who can provide you with a good life."

Deciding he'd said enough, Abe went to the barn. He spent the next hour doing the rest of the morning chores before he hitched the horses up to his wagon. By the time he brought the wagon to the front of the cabin, Phoebe and her mother were waiting for him.

He couldn't be sure what Phoebe was thinking. Her expression didn't show any emotion. But he did experience a tinge of regret as he held her hand to help her up. This was ridiculous. He should be glad. She would be getting out of here. She'd have a better future elsewhere.

Reminding himself of this, he turned back to help her mother. To his surprise, her mother said, "You give Carl what's coming to him," and then hopped up onto the wagon.

He wasn't sure if Phoebe had told her everything he'd said but decided it didn't matter. The important thing was they weren't going to fight him. It'd be much too difficult if they refused to go into town and let Eric keep an eye on them.

He tried not to pay attention to Phoebe, who sat between him and her mother. She couldn't help how close she was sitting. There was, after all, only so much room on the seat. But just as he'd been aware of how nice and soft she was the day he took them to Travis' place, he was as much aware of her today.

He gripped the reins. He was going to give Carl what was coming to him.

As he hoped, Eric was in the jailhouse and was willing to watch Phoebe and her mother.

"Make sure they don't give Phoebe or her mother any trouble," Abe whispered to Eric, nodding toward Benny and Enoch, who were sitting in their cells.

Eric assured him he'd keep Phoebe and her mother in the small room where they would be safe from them.

Thanking him, Abe left the jailhouse, not bothering to look at the men in the cell. It still burned him when he thought of the way they'd treated Phoebe. If either one of them made eye contact with him, he'd be likely to do something to make Eric lose faith in him.

When he was back on the wagon and heading out toward Carl's place, he was able to release his breath. He wasn't even aware he'd been holding it. It was much easier to deal with things when he didn't have someone to worry about.

By the time he pulled his wagon up to Carl's cabin, he heard some yelling. If he was right, Carl and his wife were arguing. Abe wasn't privy to Carl's private life. Nor did he care about it. His main concern was getting that stream and acreage. Making sure his gun was secure in the holster, he set the brake and got down from the wagon. Something shattered from inside the cabin, and Abe reconsidered talking to Carl.

But then the door flung open, and Carl, who had his back turned to Abe, yelled, "You're not so great either, Lydia! Go on back to the bottle. At least you sleep when you're drunk."

Carl slammed the door and turned to head down the steps. He paused as soon as he saw Abe. His eyes grew wide, and he glanced back at the house where his wife was still yelling something about what a "no good excuse for a husband" he was.

For a moment, Abe felt a little sorry for Carl. The gash on the side of Carl's head was proof it'd been Lydia who'd thrown the object that had shattered, and blood was trickling down his cheek. But the sympathy only lasted a moment. Who knew what Carl had done to deserve the injury?

Abe crossed the distance to him, opting not to put his hand on the revolver at his side. Carl wasn't armed, and that being the case, he didn't pose a threat. "I'm taking that stream and twenty acres," Abe told Carl, not bothering to wait for him to speak. "The judge is due here in three weeks, and he's going to force you to give it back to me. You sending for Phoebe isn't going to change anything."

Carl didn't answer right away. Instead, he reached into his back pocket and pulled out the handkerchief. He wiped the blood from the side of his face. "I need that property, Abe."

"I need it more. More than that, my uncle was here first, and he claimed it. It's mine."

"You got a well that never dries out, and it's closer to your cabin."

"That's not the point. You look at that stream, and all you think about is how much gold's in there."

Carl rolled his eyes. "Not this again."

When Carl walked around him, Abe followed him to the barn. "If you're so tired of hearing me, give me what's rightfully mine, and I'll go away."

"Your ma signed the stream over to Pa to do what he saw fit with it, and he gave it to me in the will. Not you."

"My mother lost her wits after my uncle died, and your father took advantage of that. You know it wasn't a fair deal."

As they entered the barn, Carl turned to face him. "He was your father, too. Whether we like it or not, we're related. I don't like what Pa did any more than you do. Your mother didn't lose her wits. She knew what she was doing. She let him into her bed knowing full well he was a married man."

"She had no choice," Abe snapped. "You white men come in and take everything you want without asking. What was she supposed to do? Say no and let him rape or kill her?"

Carl let out a bitter laugh and wiped more blood from his face. "Rape her? He didn't rape her. He loved her. It wasn't easy growing up knowing he'd rather be with your mother instead of mine, and it wasn't easy growing up in your shadow." He pointed to Abe's wagon, his expression dark. "That property is the one good thing Pa gave me, and I'm keeping it."

"No, you're not!"

Carl shoved him, and Abe fell onto his back. But Abe quickly rose to his feet and lunged for Carl. Carl grunted and landed on a pile of hay he'd gathered to feed his horses. Before Carl had time to get up, Abe grabbed him by the collar.

"You can't imagine all the hardships my family went through to come here. And my uncle died protecting that land and my mother. All you white men do is steal whatever you want. But I'm not letting you use that property to satisfy your greed."

Carl swung at him, but Abe lifted his arm and blocked the punch. With a grunt, Carl swept his leg under Abe. Abe failed to react fast enough and tripped, pulling Carl with him so that both landed on the floor. Carl pushed Abe away and scrambled to his feet.

"Greed?" Carl spat. "You want to talk about greed? You and your mother stole my pa from me and my ma." This time he managed to punch Abe.

Ignoring the sting of pain in his jaw, Abe swung back, his fist landing right on Carl's nose. He was about to get in another punch when a bullet fired through the air.

Both men stopped fighting and looked at the entrance of the barn. Lydia held a rifle up to her eye, and Abe couldn't tell if she was aiming it at him or Carl.

"Both of you stop acting like children and get up," she said, the breeze blowing her disheveled red hair around her face.

Abe shoved Carl back onto the floor then stood up. When he noticed she was aiming the gun at him, he walked up to her and stopped, giving her a clear shot. "If you're going to shoot, get it over with."

To his surprise, she lowered the gun and laughed. "Why would I do that? You make my husband miserable."

Abe glanced back at Carl, who hadn't bothered to get up from the floor. Instead, Carl refused to look at either one of them as he wiped his bloody nose. He knew Carl didn't have a good marriage, but until today, he'd underestimated just how bad things were between him and his wife.

"Get on out of here," Lydia told him, gesturing to his wagon.

Under normal circumstances, Abe would have pressed the issue about the stream and land, but given what he'd learned, something in him lost heart. He was going to get the property back. There was no denying that. But he couldn't bring himself to keep up the fight right now.

"Fine," Abe finally replied. "I'm going."

Then, without another look at either Carl or his wife, Abe headed for his wagon.

Chapter Fourteen

"No, I'm not going to ask her to speak to you," Phoebe heard Eric tell Enoch from the other room.

Phoebe shifted on the chair and glanced at her mother, who looked as if she was ready to doze off. Phoebe couldn't blame her. They'd been waiting for almost an hour, and Abe was still gone.

"I don't want to hurt her," Enoch protested. "I want to apologize."

"You scared her," Eric replied. "You can't expect her to see you."

"Well, can't you ask?"

"No. In the future, just make sure you don't do something like that again." Then, after a moment, Eric added, "To any woman. I don't care who she is. Women deserve to be treated with respect."

"I know, and I'll do that from now on. I promise."

Phoebe couldn't be sure, but she thought she heard Enoch's voice waver, as if he was trying not to cry. Maybe it was a foolish action on her part, but she rose to her feet and left the security of the small room.

She saw Eric sitting at his desk, flipping through some papers. Not far from her were three cells, two of which were occupied. One was occupied by Benny, of course, who was lying down on his cot with his eyes closed. In the other was Enoch, who was sitting on the cot with his face in his hands.

Eric glanced up at her. "Do you need something?"

Enoch looked up, and her gaze met his. He looked as if he was truly sorry for what he'd done. She had no proof of it, of course, but she figured she'd give him the opportunity to tell her what was on his mind.

Gathering her courage, she turned her attention back to Eric and said in a low voice, "I'll talk to Enoch."

Eric's eyebrows furrowed as he set the papers down. "Are you sure you want to do that?" he asked. "You don't owe it to him."

"I know I don't," she replied. She couldn't fully explain why she felt compelled to do it, except she sensed this might be a turning point for Enoch, that somehow, he'd be better for it. "I want to," she finally added.

"Alright," Eric consented. "But if he gives you any grief, let me know and I'll deal with him."

She nodded then went over to Enoch, her steps slow. It was hard not to remember the smell of alcohol on his breath and the way he'd cornered her in the store, but she pushed through the memories and stopped in front of him.

He didn't look so scary now. In fact, he seemed more like a lost boy. The alcohol had long since left his system, and though he hadn't bathed in who knew how long, he made an attempt to smooth his hair before he got on his knees in front of her.

"Miss Durbin," he said, looking up at her, "I'm sorry. Really, I am. I wish I could take back what I did. I'm not asking for your forgiveness. I just want you to know I'm going to give up drinking and live better."

She debated how to respond for several moments then decided on, "If you are truly sorry, then the best way to show me that is to do as you said. Clean up your life. Stop drinking alcohol. Be a good husband to your wife. Don't take another step back into the saloon."

"I won't. I promise. I learned the error of my ways, Miss Durbin."

Only time would tell if he meant it, but for the time being, she decided she'd give him the benefit of the doubt. "Thank you. I forgive you, Enoch."

The relief on his face touched her. Maybe being in jail had its desired effect on him. She certainly hoped so.

From the other cell, Benny snorted, but he kept his eyes closed.

Deciding to ignore Benny, she offered Enoch a smile then headed back to the small room. Her steps slowed as she passed Eric. She hesitated to ask him what was on her mind. Abe seemed to know him better than anyone else.

He glanced up from his papers. "Is there something you wish to discuss?"

Making sure her mother was still nodding off to sleep, she said, "Yes, there is. Can we do it outside where no one can hear us?"

He indicated that would be fine and followed her out of the building. "What's on your mind?"

She wasn't sure how to ask her question. Maybe it was best to just blurt it out. She took a deep then proceeded with, "Is it a mistake for me to marry Abe?" There. She said it. She exhaled and waited for him to respond.

"Do you want to marry him?"

"Yes. He's funny and nice. He's been taking good care of me and my mother. I don't see how any other man would be any better."

"If that's the case, then why are you asking me if you should marry him?"

"Given what's happened to me with Enoch and Benny, he thinks it's in my best interest to take my mother and leave."

Eric placed his hands on his hips as he considered Abe's argument. "I'll tell you my opinion, and you can do what you will. Yes, there are bad people here. Abe's had a hard life, and a lot of people will never accept him. Not only is he half-Indian, but his mother was his father's mistress. Those are two strikes against him, and he has no control over them. The very fact that you're associated with him is going to make things difficult for you, at least for the time being."

"But...?" Phoebe prompted, sensing there was more he wanted to say.

"But not everyone in town is bad. There are a few good people here. And the way I see it, the more good people we have here, the better our chances are of this town being a place a person can be proud to live in. Progress takes time. It's not going to happen overnight. But what if there were more people like you and your mother here? If someone bolts as soon as things get tough, they'll lose any influence they can have." He paused then nodded toward the jail. "If Enoch does as he promised you, if he cleans up his act and gets right with his wife, that will be one more person in this town who's made a change for the better. Maybe I'm too optimistic for my own good, but I like to believe things don't always have to be the way they currently are."

"I hadn't thought of it that way," Phoebe replied.

"But you shouldn't stay here just because I can see how you'd make this town a better place. You have a right to think of what's best for you and your mother. Abe has a valid concern. Life would be easier for you if you were in a more civilized place."

She thanked him and watched as he headed back into the jailhouse. He'd given her a lot to think about. She should make this decision with her head. It'd be the most sensible thing to do. But her heart unwittingly thought back to what Abe had told her earlier that morning.

It's about Carl getting his hands on gold that might or might not be in the stream. People die for gold, Phoebe. I had aunts, an uncle, and grandparents I never knew because of it. Do you honestly think I want to lose you over it, too?

He wouldn't have said that last part if he didn't care about her. People only worried about losing things they wanted to keep. Abe was willing to let her go because he believed it was in her best interest. She, however, wasn't so inclined to agree with him. Abe was a good man who'd seen more than his share of grief in life. While she couldn't begin to fully understand the pain he'd been through, she felt they belonged together.

Do you honestly think I want to lose you over it, too?

Her heart warmed as she recalled the words he'd spoken in haste. He probably wasn't aware he'd revealed his feelings for her, but she was and it stirred up emotions deep within her she'd never experienced before. Was this what love was like? She'd never been in love back in Ohio, so she had nothing to compare this feeling to. All she knew was that it was wonderful, and she didn't think she could ever feel it for anyone else.

Her mother called out her name, and Phoebe turned her attention to the entrance of the jailhouse. "What are you doing out here by yourself?" her mother asked, coming over to her.

"Oh, I wanted to talk to Eric without Enoch or Benny listening," she replied. "Ma, do you like it here?"

"You know I do."

"Even with things the way they are? With us being unable to be in town alone?"

"There are sacrifices we'd have to make wherever we go," her mother said. "No place is going to be perfect. You just need to learn to be content with wherever you are."

"And you're content here?"

"Yes, I am. I miss your brother and his family. I think of them every day. But I have you, and I've grown fond of Abe. He's a good man. I can tell he wants to marry you. He's just letting fear of being vulnerable getting in the way."

Her ears perking up, Phoebe pressed, "How can you tell he wants to marry me?"

Her mother chuckled. "A mother knows when a man takes an interest in her daughter. His gaze lingers on you longer than it should, and he's made it a point to wash up every day. He wasn't quite so tidy when we first arrived."

Do you honestly think I want to lose you over it, too? Phoebe, once again, recalled him asking earlier that day. Looking at her mother, she asked, "Is it wise to stay in a place where your safety isn't guaranteed even if you love someone?"

Her mother offered her an understanding smile and rubbed her back the way she'd often done when Phoebe was a little girl. "That's a decision only you can make." When Phoebe frowned in disappointment, her mother added, "Perhaps the better question is, is it worth it to stay in a place where you are safe if you don't love the person you're with. I'll go wherever you want, and I'll stay wherever you want. You needn't worry about me. I can be happy no matter where we are. I just want to make sure you are, too."

"I was hoping I'd get a chance to see you again!" someone called out.

Surprised, Phoebe turned in time to see an old woman hurrying over to them, a container in her arms. It was the same woman who'd waved to them on their way to see Travis last week.

The woman stopped in front of them and grinned. "I can't run as fast I used to."

"You seemed pretty fast to me," Phoebe's mother said. "I'm sure I saw you kicking up some dirt on the way here."

The woman laughed. "I like your sense of humor."

"Well, I won't stop having one until I'm in the grave," her mother replied.

"Me neither. And I'm in no hurry to go there. I got my best days ahead of me."

"I do, too. This is my daughter, Phoebe, and I'm Vivian. You can call me Viv."

"I'm Lois."

"Nice to meet you, Lois."

Phoebe followed the sentiment with a greeting of her own just as Eric came back out of the jailhouse.

"Good to see you, Lois," Eric said. "I was going to suggest Abe take these two ladies to meet you when he came back, but I see you beat me to it."

"Oh, I had nothing else to do, and I got all these cookies that need to be eaten." Lois lifted the lid, and Phoebe smelled the freshly baked goodies. "I usually make some for Eric, but I don't think he'll mind." She gave him a wink.

He chuckled. "No, I don't mind at all. But maybe we ought to go inside." He looked at Phoebe and her mother. "I think Abe would feel better if you were in that little room off to the side of my office when he comes back."

"He's right," Phoebe's mother said. "Besides, it'd be more comfortable if we're sitting as we get better acquainted."

"Lead the way," Lois replied.

Phoebe's mother did as she asked, and Phoebe went next, followed by Eric. Maybe meeting Lois was a sign. Maybe things would be alright in this town, after all. Feeling much better, Phoebe decided she'd marry Abe. The only problem, of course, was convincing him to say yes when the preacher arrived.

Chapter Fifteen

Abe stared up at Phoebe in disbelief. He'd been milking the cow when she came in to announce the preacher had arrived, ready to marry them. And he was so shocked he couldn't speak. Letting go of the teats, he rose to his feet and walked over to the entrance of the barn to make sure she was telling the truth, that the preacher was really there.

Sure enough, the old man, who'd been trying to get him to attend a church service every time he came into town, was waiting for him on the porch of the cabin. At the moment, he had his hat in hand as he talked to Phoebe's mother.

Abe turned back to face Phoebe, who hadn't moved from her spot. "I don't understand," he finally said. "Why did you tell him you wanted him to marry us?"

"Because I think we would both benefit from the arrangement," she replied, her tone so matter-of-fact it was as if it was the most logical thing they could do.

"How does it benefit you to be surrounded by scraps of metal and to have someone watch you every time you go to town? You're not safe here."

"I'm safe with you."

"You're safe until someone kills me. The moment I'm gone, you're vulnerable." He glanced at the porch. "Your mother will be vulnerable, too."

"I had time to think about it," she began, her hands clasped in front of her, "and I've decided you'll teach me and my ma how to shoot a gun. That way, we can protect ourselves if we need to."

"You've decided I'll teach you?"

He didn't know whether to laugh or be impressed. While it was funny she assumed he'd jump at the chance to teach her and her mother how to shoot a gun, he had to admit she'd taken the time to plan out her argument.

"Maybe 'decided' isn't the right word," she said. "I know you might not agree to do it, but it would be the easiest solution to my problem. And if my mother and I stay here, that will take care of your problem."

He furrowed his eyebrows. "I don't have a problem."

"Yes, you do. You have no one to help with the house or laundry, and you could use some help with the garden and cooking the meat. I'm not afraid to get my hands dirty. And best of all, I'm a quick learner."

"Tending to the garden is one thing, but you haven't seen how much goes into skinning an animal and preserving everything possible. The blood alone would make a lady with your background faint." Even his mother, who'd grown up hunting animals, had claimed illness when it came to cutting the meat, which was why he'd learned to do it at an early age.

"You don't know it'd make me faint," Phoebe argued. "You need to give me a chance to prove myself. I can do it."

He was ready to protest but caught the determined spark in her eye. He knew what that look meant. He'd seen it when his uncle had set his mind to something, and the only thing that had ever stopped his uncle was a gunshot in the chest.

So talking to her would be pointless. She had her mind set, even though she didn't have the faintest idea what she was asking. Well, maybe that should change. Up to now, he'd withheld any of the harder chores from her. Maybe if he gave her what she wanted, maybe if she got to experience just how tough the chores could be, maybe then she'd give up on this idea of being his wife.

"Alright," he finally said.

Her eyes widened in surprise. "Alright?"

She obviously hadn't expected her argument to work, at least not so soon. For all he knew, she had other arguments ready to go, just in case he continued to fight her. If she was anything like his uncle, giving up would have to be her idea.

"Yes, alright," he said. "When you see just how difficult things are, let me know, and I'll release you from the marriage."

"But you can't release me from it. We'll state our vows before man and God."

"If I recall the ways of the white man correctly, a marriage isn't final until its consummated, and I'm not going to do that until you prove you mean it, that you can do all the things you're promising to. You know, making things easier for me around here."

He could tell she wasn't thrilled with the idea of delaying the confirmation of their marriage, but it was the deal he was making. She could take it or leave it.

In a move that surprised him, she straightened her shirtwaist and lifted her chin in the air. "I can do everything I said I would."

Now his interest was piqued. "Then you'll have no trouble setting a trap and skinning an animal."

"Not as long as you teach me how to use a gun."

"Don't expect to be able to shoot your target on the first try."

"And don't expect me to skin the animal perfectly on my first try."

He felt a smile itching to turn his lips up, but he quickly suppressed it. Yes, she was a lot like his uncle, and he couldn't help but admire that about her. But he wasn't going to let her win so easily. It took more than words to prove whether or not she would be able to do it. Talk was cheap. The white man talked big all the time. But whether or not they'd follow through was the important thing. It'd be interesting to see if she was one who honored her word.

"Since you're determined to go through with this, lead the way." He waved her toward the porch.

She headed for the barn entrance and had just passed him when she turned back to him. "You just wait and see, Abe Thomas. I'll be the best wife you'll ever have."

Before he could respond, she left the barn and went to the preacher and her mother. Her mother looked much too excited about the wedding, and Abe wondered if he was only setting the poor woman up for heartache when Phoebe finally admitted she couldn't handle life out here. He forced aside the thought. He'd done all he could to avoid hurting either of them. If Phoebe was getting her mother's hopes up, then it was her fault.

Feeling more like a wolf heading for a trap than a groom about to take a wife, Abe trudged to the cabin. This was one of the most ridiculous things he'd ever done. Who ever heard of a man being married to a woman until she decided she'd had enough of him and left?

When he finally reached them, the preacher held out his hand toward Abe. "Congratulations," he said, beaming from ear to ear.

Abe glanced at his hand before he shook it. "Isn't it a little soon to congratulate me?"

"You're right. I should wait until after the bride says 'I do,'" he replied then chuckled.

No, he should wait a month or two from now and see if the bride had decided to stick around.

The preacher turned to Phoebe and her mother. "Would you like to go inside or do the ceremony out here?"

"Can we do it out here?" Phoebe glanced around and then motioned to the section of wildflowers by the garden. "Maybe over there? I think it's pretty."

Pretty? Those things grew like weeds all over the place. He had a heck of a time keeping them out of the garden.

"If it's alright with you," the preacher turned to Abe, "we'll do it over there."

Abe shrugged in response. What did he care? It wasn't like this was a real wedding. They could do this in the barn for all he cared.

The preacher and Phoebe's mother headed for the wildflowers. Not deterred in the least by his lack of enthusiasm, Phoebe took Abe's hand and urged him to follow them. With a sigh, Abe forced his feet into motion. If it'd been anyone but Phoebe, he didn't think they could have talked him into this. But since it was Phoebe, he found himself complying much too easily. It had to be those curtains. Something about those stupid things stirred up something inside him he didn't like. And when she was holding his hand, it was more intense. Something inside of him liked all of this far too much.

Determined not to dwell on it, he forced his mind on all the work he needed to do in the garden. On second thought, he'd let her do it. Might as well get her started on her new life as soon as possible. There was no sense in delaying the inevitable.

"It does my heart good to join two people who are in love," the preacher said.

Two people who are in love? Was the man daft?

The preacher smiled at him and Phoebe then added, "I've been marrying people for over thirty years, and I can always tell how a couple feels, even if they don't know it." Then, to Abe's horror, the preacher winked at him.

Wishful thinking. That's what the preacher was experiencing. It was only his desire to marry couples in love that made him believe he and Phoebe had such feelings for each other. Content with this line of reasoning, Abe gave in and listened as the man rambled on about staying together for better or worse, richer or poorer, in sickness and in health for as long as they both lived.

Abe wondered if the preacher had any idea how many white people broke these vows. There were several people he could think of off the top of his head who thought little of them. And even he was the product of such a thing. Had it not been for his father committing adultery, he wouldn't even be here.

At one point, he thought to tell the preacher these words he made him and Phoebe repeat were pointless, that they meant nothing, that it was so much like the white man to promise something and not do it. But what good would it have done?

When the preacher finished, he said, "You may kiss your bride, Abe."

It was on the tip of Abe's tongue to say such formalities were unnecessary, but Phoebe stood up on her tiptoes and kissed him before he had time to protest. Thankfully, she had the sense to make it quick. It was embarrassing enough others were watching them, but it was even more annoying that a part of him liked it.

"Now, I'll say congratulations," the preacher said, turning to him and, once more, shaking his hand.

Abe resisted the urge to grumble under his breath that this was all a waste of time.

"Well, why don't you come on in for some coffee and a piece of pie?" Phoebe's mother asked the preacher.

"I would be honored," the preacher said. He looked at Abe. "Maybe now you won't mind coming to hear a sermon since you won't have to come alone," he whispered to Abe.

"You realize most of the people you preach to don't do what you say," Abe whispered in return, deciding not to keep quiet on this matter. He'd done good enough to keep silent through the vows.

"It's my job to instruct," he replied. "What people do with the instructions is up to them." He gave him a friendly pat on the shoulder. "God doesn't care how you came to be here, Abe. He's not like them."

Abe caught Phoebe watching the exchange between them and grew uncomfortable. "I need to get back to the cow," he told the preacher. "She doesn't like it when I make her wait too long to milk her."

Without waiting for anyone to respond, he went back into the barn.

"ABE'S NEVER BEEN ONE to express his feelings," the preacher said as he hung up his hat on the hook by the door.

Phoebe led him and her mother to the kitchen table. "You two sit, and I'll get everything."

While they took a seat, she glanced out the window, and sure enough, Abe was still in the barn. Taking a deep breath, she smoothed her sweaty hands on her skirt then retrieved the coffee cups. Her hands shook, and she prayed no one noticed. It'd taken considerable effort to get through the ceremony. But she'd done it.

She'd convinced Abe to give her a chance to prove he'd benefit from having her out here. And she was going to prove it. Just wait until he realized how serious she was. Sure, she grew up in a more civilized place, but that didn't mean she couldn't handle it out here. It was just a matter of determination.

She managed to pour coffee into three cups without spilling it, which was good considering her hands shook. Then she cut a slice of the fresh peach pie and put it on the plate for the preacher.

"Ma, do you want one?" she asked, looking over at her mother, who was still talking the poor preacher's ear off about Phillip and his family.

"I don't like to spoil my supper, so I'll just have a small piece," her mother replied.

Phoebe nodded and cut out a small slice for her mother.

"Phillip married in a church," her mother was telling the preacher. "But back in Cincinnati, that was an easy thing to do. There are a lot of them there. It's not like out here where we have to wait for someone like you to come in. A church wedding is nice, but I have to say watching my daughter marry outside with the sunlight streaming through the trees and lighting up the area around us, was a breathtaking sight. I can't recall a time I'd seen anything so beautiful."

"This is a beautiful territory," the preacher began, "though it does have its hardships. I've seen my share of tragedy." He sighed for a moment, as if reliving one or two events from his past. But then he smiled again and continued, "I've also seen some miracles. Not all of them are big ones. Most are small. So small, in fact, it'd be easy to mistake them for common occurrences."

Phoebe placed the cups in front of them.

She was ready to bring them their slices of pie when the preacher made eye contact with her and said, "Abe getting married was nothing short of a miracle. That poor man hasn't had anyone who's cared anything about him since his ma died five years ago. He lost his uncle when he was only ten. It was just him and his ma after that, and she was weak so he had to grow up fast and take over the care of this place. It'll be nice for him to have someone to help him." He smiled at Phoebe. "Don't let him fool you. He wouldn't have married you if he didn't want to. There's no making Abe do anything he doesn't want to. I don't care how much someone argues with him. That boy is as stubborn as a mule."

"It's because he's stubborn that he's managed out here as well as he has," her mother said after she took a sip of her coffee.

"Yes, it is," he acknowledged. "It's the only way anyone can stick it out this far from civilization. This kind of life isn't for the faint of heart, I'll tell you that. You two are brave ladies to be out here."

"I don't know if being brave has anything to do with it," her mother said. "We had no money, and my son was struggling to make ends meet. Phoebe answered a mail-order bride ad to find someone who could support us. When we first came here, we thought we'd made the trip for nothing. It turned out another person posted that mail-order bride ad on Abe's behalf, and Abe didn't know about it."

The preacher glanced over at Phoebe as she set the plates full of pie and forks in front of him and her mother. "Why would someone do that?"

Since he seemed to be asking her the question, Phoebe answered, "I think it was so Abe would stop arguing with Carl Richie about the stream over there." She pointed in the direction of the stream and land. "I suppose Carl thought Abe would have more important things to worry about if my mother and I were here."

"Well," he began as he picked up his fork, "sometimes when man does something out of selfishness, God turns it around for good."

"That's what I've been thinking about this whole thing," Phoebe's mother said. "Nothing happens by accident."

"No, it doesn't. You two are here for Abe, and I have no doubt you'll be good for him. Every man, no matter how strong he thinks he is, needs people in his life who can accept him as he is."

Phoebe's gaze went back to the window. Abe was still in the barn. She had a nagging suspicion he was going to stay in there until the preacher left. And that was his right. He wasn't the type who easily welcomed people into his life, and given what she knew, she couldn't blame him. She only hoped, in time, he would allow himself the freedom to love her.

Chapter Sixteen

"What are you doing here?" Abe asked that evening after he opened his bedroom door.

Phoebe was sorting through a small pile of clothes she'd brought into his room. For the moment, the pile was gathered on the dresser.

This, however, wasn't the worst of it. She was wearing nothing but a nightshirt that reached her knees. He'd never seen so much of a woman's legs in his life, and he'd have to be dead not to let his gaze linger on them. Bringing his gaze up, he was aware the lack of layers only emphasized the curve of her breasts.

He blinked and forced his attention to a far more pressing matter, which happened to be the fact she was moving into his bedroom, the only safe place he had in this cabin.

"Why aren't you in your room?" he asked.

"We're married," Phoebe said in the same matter-of-fact tone she'd used earlier that day in the barn. She took one of the dresses and turned to the armoire. "This is my room now."

"I thought I made it clear we aren't doing anything." He gestured to the bed when she glanced at him. "In there."

"You did. I know we're not doing anything tonight."

"Not just tonight. I mean, *ever*."

"No, it's just until you feel confident I can do everything that's required of me to stay here." She hung up another dress. "Nothing can happen between us tonight anyway. The lady's time is upon me."

It took him a moment to realize she meant she was on her monthly cycle. "Well, even when you're done with it, we're not doing anything."

"Not right away."

He fought back the urge to groan. What was wrong with her? Did it really please her to argue with him?

"I can't sleep in the other bedroom," she added. "My mother will ask questions, and I'd rather not answer them. I know we made a deal, but I don't feel like explaining it to her."

As much as he wanted to keep arguing, he couldn't. He couldn't blame her for not wanting to tell her mother what they'd agreed to. It was complicated enough without dragging an innocent party into it. But still...

"What are you going to tell her when things don't work out, and you head on out of here?" he asked.

"That's not going to happen," she replied. "So, you see, telling her anything would be pointless anyway."

She turned to face him as if daring him to argue with her, but even if he'd wanted to, he couldn't. When she had turned to him, she'd given him a much better view of her breasts, which were barely concealed under the thin fabric of her nightshirt. And worse, he could make out the tips of her nipples.

"Well, if you're going to sleep in here, I'm going to sleep in the loft," he finally decided.

Her eyes grew wide. "That doesn't make any sense."

"It makes perfect sense," he said as he grabbed a fresh pair of undergarments and shirt.

Lady's time of month or not, she couldn't expect him to keep his hands off of her if she was in bed with him. Drifting off to sleep in the loft was one thing. She'd been fully dressed, and it'd been an accident. This was on purpose, and she was practically naked. She probably had no idea what effect she was having on him, but he was only human and could only handle so much.

"Are you going to spend every night in the loft?" she asked.

"Yep, until you're on the stagecoach."

Ignoring her bewildered expression, he left the room and headed out for the barn. At least the night was a chilly one. That should go a long way in cooling his ardor. He had to show her just how hard life was out here. The sooner he did, the easier things would be.

RIGHT AFTER BREAKFAST the next morning, Abe wiped his mouth with a cloth napkin then set it on the table. Looking at Phoebe, he asked, "Are you ready to set a trap?" before Phoebe had a chance to pick up anything to help her mother wash the dishes.

"Set the trap?" Phoebe replied.

"You said you were willing to learn how to do it."

Noting the challenge in his eyes, she said, "I wasn't trying to back out of doing it. I just thought I'd help my ma clean up first." She motioned to the dirty dishes.

"Oh, don't mind me," her mother spoke up. "I can do these. You go on and set the trap."

"Alright." Phoebe headed for the bedroom she now shared with Abe, but she stopped and glanced at him. "I'm going to braid my hair so it doesn't get in my way," she told him before he could think she was going to do something like crawl out the window and hide.

Since he didn't reply, she figured she'd made her point and went to the bedroom. It was going to take more than a simple trap to intimidate her. Once she had her hair braided, she came back out, surprised he'd taken the time to take the dishes over to the sink so her mother could wash them.

She bit her tongue and waited until they left the cabin before saying, "For someone who's eager to get rid of me, you're being awfully nice to my mother."

He frowned. "I don't understand what your mother has to do with this."

"My mother has everything to do with this. I refused to leave her behind in Ohio because I can't imagine my life without her. One of my requirements in marrying was that my husband be good to her."

He snorted. "I'm not going to treat your mother badly. I don't need to. Once you see how difficult this life is, you'll be out of here."

She decided to let his comment go. He was determined things would play out this way, and arguing about it would accomplish nothing. Abe was the kind of person who needed to see it to believe it. And she'd show it to him.

When they arrived in the barn, he grabbed a folded up blanket, a pair of gloves, a handheld digging tool, and a small trap. "Open your arms," he said.

Surprised, she did as he requested and he dumped everything in them.

"If you're going to do this, you're going to do all of it. I won't be doing anything but telling you what to do."

"Oh, good. I wouldn't want you to make it too easy," she quipped, refusing to let him deter her. "I'm likely to get bored if there's not enough challenge." She headed out of the barn then asked, "Will we be going to the spot you put your trap the other day?"

"No. You'll be doing this with unused ground. That's why you're taking that trowel."

"Trowel?"

He pointed to the handheld digging tool.

"Is that what you call it?" she asked, surprised. "I thought it was a little shovel."

She noted his lips curl up into a smile despite his attempt to look serious. "I suppose that works, too," he said.

For the rest of their trek up into the trees, they were quiet until he came to a large tree stump.

He turned to her and gestured for her to put everything down. "You can set the trap here."

"We're on an incline," she replied.

"Yes, but we're also along a frequented trail. See the animal prints? They go in a line down through here."

She followed his gaze and saw that, sure enough, there were prints along the path. "I didn't notice those around the traps you set. Were they there, too?"

"Yes. You'll have to start paying attention to details if you're going to live here."

With a nod, she put the things on the ground. "What do I do first?"

"First you put down the blanket."

She inspected it, suddenly noticing the dirt on it. "Hmm..."

"'Hmm' what?"

"It's filthy," she said.

"I rub it in the leaves and dirt to hide my scent when I use it. In this case, we'll be masking your scent."

"I have a scent?" she asked, not sure if she believed him or not. For all she knew, he could be teasing her.

"Every living thing has a scent, even people. You can smell some white men in town a mile away from the alcohol on their breaths. But it's more pleasant to smell women, especially ones like..."

Since he stopped, she encouraged him to continue. She couldn't be sure, but she thought he blushed a little as he waved her question aside.

"It doesn't matter," he said. "What's important is that you sit on that blanket when you set the trap."

Realizing she wasn't going to get her answer, she unfolded the blanket and set it on the ground. Afterwards, she turned to him. "Now what?"

"Put on the gloves."

She did and quickly realized they were too big for her.

"If you actually end up staying, I'll get you a pair better suited for you."

"Oh good. I want mine to be pink," she joked and knelt on the blanket. "I'm guessing this is where I put the trap down?"

"Not yet."

He knelt next to her, and she couldn't help but note how close they were. Recalling his comment on how people had their own scent, she noticed he had a nice smell about him. He smelled rugged, just like the outdoors. Now whenever she smelled this particular scent, she'd think of him.

"Dig a hole big enough to put this trap in." He lifted the trap and set it down in front of her to show her how big it should be. "After you dig it, you'll set the trap then put it in the hole. After that, you'll cover it up with the leaves and dirt you dug up."

That sounded simple enough. Moving aside the trap, she dug the hole, careful to put the dirt, leaves and small twigs to the side for easy access. When she was done, she put the trowel down and peered up at him.

"Are you going to show me how to set the trap, or do I need to figure that out myself?" she asked.

"I'll tell you what to do," he replied. "You have to be careful with these things. One wrong move could leave you with a broken finger or thumb."

She snickered. "You're trying to scare me."

"No, I'm not." He picked up the trap. "This is the free jaw." He lifted one of the jaws and moved it back and forth. "It's the part that catches the animal and holds it in place. The other jaw is fixed." He pointed to the other one. "It doesn't move. This is how you set the trap."

She watched as he snapped the free jaw in place. Then, making sure his fingers weren't in the way, he released the trap. She jumped when it snapped shut.

"That's why you have to be careful," he said. "If you make the wrong move, you could hurt yourself. Think you got the idea, or should I show you again?"

"I think I can do it." She took it from him and repeated the process, surprised it was as easy as it looked. Once she set it in the hole, she couldn't resist teasing him. "At what point am I supposed to get squeamish and run for the next stagecoach?"

As she'd hoped, the corner of his lip turned up. He, however, forced the stern expression back on his face. "Just wait until you have to get the animal out and skin it. That's when things get tough." He nodded toward the pile of dirt and leaves. "Go on and hide the trap."

She proceeded to do so, taking care to keep the trap set. When she was done, she got up and gathered the blanket and trowel. "Are you going to teach me how to shoot a gun?"

"I said I would, and I will."

"Good. I wouldn't want you to wiggle your way out of our deal."

"I stay true to my word. I do not practice the ways of the white man."

"Well, I'm going to show you a white woman can, and will, keep her word. You'll be surprised, Abe. I just know it."

"I can tell you're determined, but there's a difference between being determined and being able to do the work."

"That's why you'll be surprised. You're going to learn you can't put limits on me."

"Were you this stubborn in Ohio?"

"No, but then I didn't need to be. As you pointed out, life out here will be hard. In order to stay, I have to be willing to do whatever it takes to survive. I'm not afraid of doing any of it. I just need to learn what I need to do."

She caught the spark of respect in his eyes but chose not to comment. Even if Abe didn't say it, she sensed he was glad she was as determined as she was to stick around. He hadn't protested all that hard when she moved into his bedroom, and those curtains were still hanging up. If he really didn't want her there, he would have protested harder.

Nope. She suspected the truth was, he was hoping she would prove him wrong. And she would. The only question was, how long was it going to take for her to do it.

Chapter Seventeen

After a light lunch, Abe took Phoebe to the barn and handed her a revolver. Phoebe frowned as she turned the gun over in her hands.

"What's wrong?" he asked, checking to make sure there were enough bullets in the sack.

"I thought it'd be bigger," she said. She gestured to the gun rack on the wall. "Like that one."

His gaze went to the rifle before he looked back at her. "It's not the size of the gun that matters. It's how well you handle what you got."

She didn't seem all that pleased with what he said but continued to examine it.

"It'll be better for you to learn on a smaller gun," he assured her. "When you first shoot, you'll probably jerk back a little. Better to do that with the Colt than a rifle."

"But I thought you didn't want to make things easy for me," she said.

He wouldn't have laughed, except her eyebrows were raised in a challenge. Once he managed to settle the urge to chuckle, he told her, "It's a matter of convenience. If you wish to start with the larger gun, by all means, do so."

She drummed her fingers on the gun, and he could tell she was weighing the pros and cons of getting the rifle. In the end, good sense won out when she said, "Alright. I'll use this one. I might be eager to learn, but I don't want to be foolish about it."

"When you realize those things aren't as easy as they look, you'll be glad you started small."

From there, he led her out of the barn and down a ways from the cabin where he had set up targets. He put up a couple of bottles along the posts of an old fence his uncle had set up.

He went back over to her. "Don't expect to hit your target on the first try. You have six shots until you need more bullets, so you might as well start practicing. But first, you need to know how to stand. Spread your feet apart like this."

He demonstrated by setting his feet about twelve inches apart.

"Do they have to be exactly that far apart?" she asked.

"As far apart as you're comfortable with. I don't think this," he spread his legs as far apart as they would go, "would be comfortable." Noting her laughter, he added, "And you might even fall." He got back into a comfortable stance. "Just whatever's comfortable is fine."

"Alright." She spread her legs apart, her long skirt swirling around her boots. "Do I start shooting?"

"Not yet. Hold onto the gun with both hands, and lift it up so it's about eye level. Keep your arms and wrists firm. There's going to be a kickback when you fire, so keeping your arms and wrists firm will help buffer you from it," he added, figuring she'd want to know why. She was, after all, curious by nature.

She glanced his way.

It took him a moment to understand she was asking if there was anything else she needed to know before she started shooting. "Shoot whenever you're ready," he said.

With a nod, she turned her focus back to the bottle directly in front of her. She took a deep breath then released it. He expected her to fire the gun, but she hesitated. He hid his smile. She was so intent on doing a good job on her first try. Yep, she was a lot like his uncle. His uncle would have liked her. *She might be white, but she has the heart of a Cherokee,* his uncle would have said.

Abe forced the thought aside. He couldn't be distracted. She'd asked him to teach her how to shoot a gun, and since she'd graciously set the trap that morning, he would fulfill his part of the deal.

She finally pulled the trigger. As he'd expected, she missed the bottle. What he hadn't expected, however, was the fact that she let out a surprised shriek.

She rubbed her wrists and shook her arms. "I didn't think that'd happen. Does the gun always push back when you shoot?"

"What did you think I meant when I told you there would be a kickback?"

After a moment, she shrugged. "I'd never heard the term before, so I didn't know. I figured I'd experience it for myself when the time came."

"Well, you did experience it."

She blinked, as if she didn't expect his answer. Then she laughed. "Yes, I suppose I did. Is there anything else I should expect?"

"I think that's it, but if you actually hit one of those bottles today, I'll be shocked."

"How long will you let me try?"

"Until you're bored or until your ma rings the dinner bell. One thing we'll be doing, though, is filling the chamber of that gun with more bullets. A shooting match does you no good if you can't load up an empty gun."

She gasped, her eyes growing wide. "You have gunfights out here?"

"This is the West. Anything goes. It's why I'm pushing so hard for you to get out of here. Find a good, civilized place and live a peaceful life."

For a brief moment, he thought his warning was finally getting through to her. But then that spark flashed in her eyes and she straightened her posture, as if daring anyone to come right out of the trees and start shooting her right here on the spot.

"I can do it," she said. "A woman can fire a gun just as well as a man can, and I'll be one of the best shots in this territory."

Then, without another word, she positioned herself as he'd taught and fired off five bullets back to back. She didn't hit any of the bottles, but maybe that hadn't been her point. Her point might just have been to show him she was going to keep shooting as long as she had bullets left.

She turned to him and gestured to his bag. "Are you going to show me how to load the gun?"

Even if he found her actions a bit hasty, he couldn't help but admire her willpower. Yes, his uncle would have loved having her out here. He'd probably even lock her and Abe in the bedroom until Abe got the consummation of their marriage over with. But since his uncle wasn't here, there was no threat of that happening.

Though, would it really be so bad? Just get it over with and enjoy the feel of her soft body against him? Experience the joy of a kiss? Get to share a moment with her he'd never share with anyone else?

Snapping out of his thoughts, he opened the sack. He'd be better off tending to the lesson. He took the gun from her and showed her how to open the chamber and slip in the bullets. After he was done, he spun the chamber and handed it back to her.

"Think you can do it next time?" he asked.

"Sure," she replied. "It wasn't all that complicated." She took the gun, her fingers brushing his.

He didn't know whether to be irritated or excited. Did she do it on purpose? And if she had, would he have enjoyed it even more?

This time when she fired the gun, she didn't rush to fire the next bullet. She furrowed her eyebrows and concentrated on her aim. She waited for a few seconds, tracing her lower lip with her tongue, and then pulled the trigger. To his surprise, the bullet brushed the edge of the bottle, making it teeter for a moment before it settled back in place.

Phoebe let out a cheer and jumped up and down. "I did it! I did it!"

Since she was so excited, he didn't have the heart to tell her it didn't count unless she hit the bottle head on. For a first time with a gun, she did well, and he'd let her have her victory.

"Can you believe it?" she asked him, her smile growing wider. "I bet you didn't think I could do it."

"Not so soon," he consented.

"Well, you just wait. I proved you wrong here, and I'll prove you wrong when I catch the animal in my trap."

"Tapping a bottle and skinning an animal are two different things."

"But I'll do it. You'll see."

She turned her attention back to the bottle and resumed her lesson, and deep down, he couldn't deny the small part of him that hoped she was right.

"IT TOOK ME AN HOUR, but I finally got that bottle off the post," Phoebe told her mother during their meal that evening. "I bet Abe didn't think I'd get it done on my first day, but I did."

"To be fair," Abe interrupted as he buttered his roll, "you hadn't shot a gun before. I don't think your expectations were any higher than mine."

She paused and thought over his statement. He was right. She hadn't expected to hit the bottle on her first day of shooting, either. Inspired, she said, "That just goes to show I'm meant to be here since it came so easy."

He cocked his eyebrow but didn't argue with her.

Her mother looked up from her mashed potatoes and met her gaze. "Was it scary to shoot a gun?"

"A little," Phoebe admitted, almost hating to say it right in front of Abe. "But," and she hoped Abe would remember this part, "it got easier the more I did it."

Her mother nodded. "That's to be expected, I suppose. Anything new can be intimidating." She glanced at Abe and smiled. "It's a lot different out here than it was in Cincinnati."

"I don't doubt it," Abe replied after he swallowed the roll.

"We checked the trap I set earlier today," Phoebe said, deciding it might not be best to let him dwell on how different things were. Or, at the very least, get him to start persuading her mother to leave. "So far, the trap is empty, but maybe there'll be something there tomorrow. Then I'll learn how to get us meat to put in stews or fry up in a skillet."

Her mother's eyes widened. "Why, you weren't joking when you said you were going to learn how to do everything Abe does." She winked at Abe. "I thought she was exaggerating. I thought maybe she'd learn how to shoot a gun and tend the garden. I didn't think catching animals would be a part of it."

Abe shot Phoebe a pointed look. "There's also mucking out stalls, cleaning the horses and cow, gathering eggs—"

"And repairing the barn roof when there's a hole in it," Phoebe finished for him.

"Oh good heavens," her mother said with a chuckle. "He doesn't expect you to do all that. There are things women do and things men do. I can see gathering food if you need to. Given what happened that day in town, I can even see learning how to shoot a gun. But cleaning stalls and animals or fixing a roof are things he'll be doing."

"I can do them as well as he can," Phoebe argued.

"How are you going to have time to take care of the home and cook if you're doing all those other chores?" her mother asked, picking up a cup. "There's only so many hours in a day. Marriage is a partnership. The two work together, but they have their own tasks to do." She took a sip then chuckled. "Next thing I know, you'll be telling me he'll start sewing clothes."

Abe grimaced at the idea, and Phoebe chuckled under her breath. Maybe she should challenge him for a change. See if he could make a

new shirt. But she didn't have the heart. Besides, he had some valid reasons to be concerned about her. This was a harsher environment than
the one she'd been used to in Ohio. She had to learn how to fend for
herself, just in case it came to that. And she would. Before the year
was up, she had no doubt she'd be fully capable of doing everything he
could.

She turned her attention back to her mother. "When I get good at
shooting, I'll teach you how to do it."

Her mother coughed on the food she'd been swallowing. Just as
Phoebe was ready to get up and pat her back, her mother was back to
normal. She took a drink of her coffee and shook her head. "Did I hear
you right? You expect me to shoot a gun?"

"Why not?" Phoebe asked. "It's not a bad idea."

"Well, I," her mother paused then continued, "I'm old."

"You're not too old to do this. Besides, you came all the way out
here with me. Shooting a gun isn't as hard as sitting in a train or getting
tossed about a stagecoach for days on end."

"Tossed about?" Abe asked.

Phoebe nodded. "We thought we were going to bump the ceiling
when we hit the ruts in the road."

"Thankfully, we were blessed with sturdy stomachs," her mother
added. "The driver told us about a woman who couldn't stop throwing
up for days." She shivered. "We were relieved we didn't have to share it
with her. The man and wife we were with for most of the trip also had
healthy constitutions."

"Yes, we did luck out," Phoebe agreed.

"I wouldn't want to take a child on such a trip," her mother said.
"It's hard enough on adults."

"Which is why we're staying right where we are." Phoebe glanced at
Abe then, and she wasn't surprised when he lifted his gaze heavenward.
"Besides, we both like it here, don't we, Ma?"

"We do. Abe, you've been very kind to us. Thank you."

Abe turned his gaze to Phoebe, so Phoebe offered him her most charming smile.

She thought she caught a flicker of pleasure as he shook his head at her, but his expression quickly went neutral. Abe had a way of being able to mask his feelings. She was quickly learning she had to pay attention to his face right away after she said or did something to gauge what he was trying to hide. And she was sure she saw that little spark of pleasure. So sure, in fact, she'd stake her life on it. With a smile, she got up to give everyone a slice of pie.

Chapter Eighteen

The next day after finding nothing in the animal trap, Abe figured he might as well show Phoebe how to maintain the garden. The task was simple enough. All she had to do was pull some weeds and get rid of insects that could harm the growing plants. It wasn't quite the task that would have her running off for a stagecoach, but it was part of living out here so she might as well get familiar with it.

As she was watering the plants, he heard the scraps of metal clinking together. Without hesitation, he bolted for the barn. He shouldn't have let his guard down. He should've remembered it was important to carry a gun at all times. Phoebe was far too distracting.

He grabbed the Colt and hurried out of the barn. He would have peeked out the window had Phoebe not been standing out there in plain sight for anyone to see. By the time he made it to the garden, he saw old lady Lois bringing her well-used buggy up the path to their house.

Relaxing, he set the gun at his side.

"Do you usually have dangerous people coming out here during the day?" Phoebe asked, coming over to him.

"No." He slipped the gun into his back pocket. "But you can't be too careful."

"Lois and my mother got along really well the other day in town," Phoebe said, smiling as the old lady continued leading the horse up the property. "It's nice Ma finally has someone her own age to talk to."

"She didn't have that in Ohio?"

"None she felt close to."

Phoebe left his side and ran over to greet Lois. Abe stood there for a moment, just watching as Phoebe talked to Lois. The front door of the cabin opened, and her mother let out an excited cry when she saw their visitor.

As mother and daughter helped Lois out of the buggy, Abe shook his head. There was no way Phoebe was leaving now. Not since they had befriended someone as nice as Lois, one of the few white people who'd always looked Abe right in the eye and said hi to him, no matter how many people in town saw her do it. Lois was a gutsy lady, too. No doubt, she had a gun somewhere in that buggy with her.

Her husband had been a tough man. Very protective of her, but also fair to all he came across, including Abe's uncle. He'd taken it upon himself to bury his uncle and had checked in on Abe and his mother from time to time. Abe still missed him, though he'd often felt better knowing that dying in one's sleep was the best way a man could go.

"Well, Abe, don't be a stranger," Lois called out to him as she turned from Phoebe and her mother. "Come on over."

He did as she wanted, and though it was embarrassing to be hugged as if he were a child, he hugged Lois back, knowing it would hurt the poor woman's feelings if he didn't.

"It's nice to see you taking a wife," Lois told him. "The preacher was grinning from ear to ear about it at the sermon this morning." She glanced at Phoebe and her mother. "I know it's not Sunday, but he likes to have a sermon every day he's here to make up for the Sundays we miss."

"Oh, we didn't realize that," Phoebe's mother said. "He didn't say a word to us about it yesterday while he was here."

"I'm sure you had more important things going on, what with the wedding and all," Lois replied.

"It was a lovely ceremony." Her mother gestured to the flowers. "We all stood over there. I'm telling you, it was much nicer than being inside."

"As long as it's not too hot or cold or windy, outside is always best."

"I just finished making some tarts. Would you like one?"

"That'd be lovely."

Phoebe's mother turned to Abe and Phoebe. "You want to come, too?"

"No, I need to keep working," Phoebe said.

"Oh, we don't need to bother them," Lois told Phoebe's mother with a wink. "The two are newlyweds. They have better things to do than hang around us old folk."

Phoebe's mother giggled and led Lois into the cabin.

Despite the breeze, Abe could feel his face warming as he considered what he could be doing with Phoebe instead of showing her how to care for a garden.

Phoebe clasped her hands in front of her and turned to face him. "Is it wise to have the gun ready for when someone comes onto this property?"

Relieved she hadn't been able to tell the direction his thoughts had taken, he said, "I like to be prepared. You never know what will happen."

"Then should I wear a gun in the holster you gave me?" When he furrowed his eyebrows, she added, "In case I'm not near the barn, I can have it."

"Now that you know how to shoot one, it's probably a good idea. But we have some in the house, too. I keep a couple in the drawer in the nightstand."

"I don't recall seeing one when I put my things in your bedroom."

"They were on my side under my things."

"Oh." She nodded and let out a sigh. "Is there anything else I should do with the garden?"

"No. We're done with that for the day."

"Good. Should we check the trap and see if I caught an animal?"

"Yes." It'd be nice to take a short walk. "I suppose you can even practice shooting if there's nothing in the trap."

"Sure. That'll be fun."

His eyebrow raised in surprise. "Fun?"

"It's fun to see if I can shoot a bottle," she said.

"But it's not fun to shoot someone."

"I didn't say it was. I hope I never have to shoot anyone."

He studied her and saw that what she was saying was true. While she didn't want to shoot anyone, she understood there might come a day when she'd have to, and she was fully prepared for it. Yes, she had the spirit of a Cherokee in her. His uncle would be asking him why he insisted on being so stubborn. *Just make her your wife already,* his uncle would say if he was alive.

Shoving the thought aside, Abe said, "I'll get your holster, and we'll head out."

Then he went to the barn.

THAT EVENING ABE SAT in the barn loft. He had waited until Phoebe's mother went to bed before coming out here. He didn't want her mother to wonder why he wasn't going to bed with Phoebe. He couldn't even explain it to himself. He was making things more difficult than he had to. That, he understood. But for the life of him, he didn't know why.

After staring at the open doorway of the barn for a while, he shook his head and got his blanket and pillow to set out for the night. He didn't know what he was waiting for. Just what did he think was going to happen? Unless he went back to the cabin, he wasn't going to see Phoebe again.

He took off his boots and blew out the light in the lantern hanging on the hook over his head. What was wrong with him? Was he really pining away for some woman like a lovesick schoolboy? The whole thing was ridiculous. Yes, she had spunk. Yes, she managed to impress him. But that didn't mean he had to fall at her feet in adoration.

Letting her know she'd done a good job was enough. She hadn't run off when the gun had offered its kickback. His mother had fired a gun once, and that was all it took for her to say she didn't care for it. Phoebe, on the other hand, not only practiced more that day, but she'd shown patience in waiting for the trap to yield an animal.

He must remember to tell her she did admirably with the chores the next time he saw her. Feeling much better, he closed his eyes and released his breath. This was his favorite time of the day. The soothing sounds of the occasional coyote, horse neighing, and crickets always had a calming effect on him. He took a deep breath and released it again, feeling the day's tension easing from his muscles. He could finally rest.

"Are you awake?"

His eyes flew open, and he bolted up, his head just barely missing the ceiling. In the dark, he barely made out Phoebe's face as she peered at him from the top of the ladder. He put his hand over his heart and gulped a breath of fresh air. How did he not hear her coming?

"You're too quiet for my own good," he told her. "Aren't you wearing anything on your feet?"

"I found a pair of your soft shoes and slipped them on. I'm sorry. I didn't mean to scare you."

He was ready to reassure her he was fine when he remembered she mentioned wearing his shoes. "Aren't my moccasins too big for your feet?"

"All I was doing was coming out here. Have you seen all the buttons on my boots? It'd take ten minutes to get all those done up right." After a moment, she asked, "Can I have a pair of moccasins? It'd be nice to have something more comfortable when I do the chores around here."

"Did you come out here to ask me that?"

"No. I just thought of that question now. I actually came out to ask if I can stay out here with you."

"Why?"

"Because it's hard to sleep alone. I got so used to being with someone. Back in Ohio, the only time I slept by myself was on a couch, and it was before my pa died. When Ma and I moved in with Phillip, we had to sleep in the same bed."

He was ready to suggest she sleep with her ma tonight, but he already knew why she couldn't. He let out a sigh as he debated whether or not this was a good idea. Yes, they had slept out here together before, but back then, she'd fallen asleep without meaning to and they hadn't been married. It'd been easier to resist doing anything.

"You can't sleep here," he told her. "I'll talk with you for a while if that's what you want, but I'm going to take you back to the cabin when you get tired."

"Why can't I sleep here?" she asked as she crawled into the loft.

He moved over, giving her enough room so she could get comfortable. "You don't know when to stop," he muttered.

After she got comfortable, she turned to face him. "All I'm doing is lying next to you."

All she was doing was lying next to him? Did she honestly believe that? He glanced at her and saw she did, in fact, mean it. The woman had no idea she was playing with fire.

"Yeah, well, don't get too comfortable," he finally said and settled onto his back.

He crossed his arms because he didn't know what to do with his hands. At least this way, they were safely tucked under each arm.

She, however, didn't help matters any when she snuggled up to him and rested her head on his shoulder.

He sighed in irritation. "What are you doing?"

"Just resting." She slipped her arm around his waist. "I can see why you like it out here. It's nice."

"I don't come out here every night."

"I know, but since you have a blanket and pillow, I figure you come out here once in a while. And this was even before my ma and I arrived on the stagecoach. How often would you sleep out here?"

"Maybe once or twice a week unless it was too cold."

"What brought you out here so often?"

"Habit."

"Habit?"

She wasn't going to quiet down any time soon. When she said she couldn't sleep, she meant it. He didn't know whether to chuckle or groan.

"What started the habit, Abe?" she asked. "You can tell me even if it's not pleasant."

"It's something I started when I was a child. This was the one place I could go to when I needed to be alone," he replied. "It was just," for lack of a better word, he shrugged, "nice."

"I had a place like that, too, when I was younger. There was a tree in the park I used to climb up. I used to pretend it was in the middle of a large jungle and-"

"You know what a jungle looks like?"

"No, but I saw a painting of one in the library. There were a couple of illustrations in some books Ma would read to me, too. I like it out here. It reminds me of a jungle, but only because there are so many trees. There aren't lots of hideous insects or snakes."

He chuckled. "Yes, there are. Maybe not the kind in jungles, but we have them out here."

She lifted her head and peered down at him, her eyes wide. "Dangerous ones?"

He considered telling her no, but what good would that be? "Some, but I don't often see them." When a worried frown crossed her pretty face, he added, "If you stay on the main paths, you'll be fine."

If he was smart, he'd tell her all sorts of tall tales about men who'd lived out here and saw their untimely demise from a black widow or a rattlesnake, but he didn't have the heart to do it. Not only would it be wrong for him to intentionally scare her, but he didn't want her to leave. It was a truth he'd been putting off long enough. There was no sense in denying it anymore.

However, that didn't mean he had to tell her. Not yet anyway. She still needed to learn to skin the animal. It was the hardest part of living out here, minus the attitude from some people in town. He had to know if she was strong enough to press through it.

His mother had been weak. His uncle had sheltered her far too much, and that was something he didn't understand until she couldn't handle it after his father died of a heart attack. For as long as he lived, he didn't think he'd get over the image of his mother lying in bed with the empty bottle of poison beside her.

She hadn't warned him. There had been no indication she was thinking of killing herself. If she'd talked to him, he didn't know if he could have talked her out of it. He'd only been sixteen. Yes, he would have tried, but her devotion to his father had run so deep it was hard to get through to her about anything.

He took a deep breath and released it, and in doing so, he brought himself into the present. Phoebe was still resting beside him. With a sigh, he brought his arm around her, and she snuggled closer to him.

"You aren't the kind of woman who needs a man in order to survive, are you?" he asked.

"What do you mean by that?"

"If something were to happen to me, you'd be able to take care of yourself and your mother, wouldn't you?"

"I thought that's why you're teaching me how to shoot a gun and provide food for us," she replied. "So that if I needed to, I could take care of everything on my own."

His eyebrows furrowed. How did she come to that conclusion? He thought she suspected he was being stubborn for the sake of being stubborn. He should have given her more credit. She was smart enough to put the pieces together.

"I just don't want you to think life out here is easy," he said.

"I know," she assured him. "I'm not expecting it to be."

"I don't understand why you want to be here so badly."

"I like being with you," she said. "And deep down, I think you like being with me, too. But that's not the only reason. I like it here. This is a nice place. My mother likes it here. She's got a friend now. There are some good people in town. If we can get more good people around here, then things are bound to get better."

The last part of her explanation made him laugh. Phoebe was quite the optimist, but sooner or later, she'd come to learn the hard truth. "Don't be fooled into thinking Eric putting Benny and Enoch in jail made any difference. The bad always finds a way to pop up, and often when you least expect it."

"That's why I'm learning to shoot a gun. If something bad happens again, I'll be able to react better than I did in the general store."

"You shouldn't have to worry about going into a general store."

"And I won't next time because I'll have a gun, and I'll know how to use it."

"Well, it's not a bad idea to be near a gun at all times. I know you think the rifle is the better choice, but it's a lot easier to carry a Colt with you wherever you go."

He felt her nod and decided that was enough warning for one evening. She was taking his words to heart, and that gave him comfort. Maybe, just maybe, she could handle living out here.

For tonight, however, it was enough to close his eyes and hold her. She settled into silence, and he could only guess what was going through her mind. He resisted the urge to ask her. Instead, he relaxed, and before long, he fell asleep.

Chapter Nineteen

Phoebe's exhilaration of catching an animal quickly gave way to apprehension as Abe placed the fox on the ground, setting it on its back. She watched as he positioned the upper half of its body on an incline.

"Why aren't we doing this in the barn?" she asked.

"Because this is your first time, and you're likely to puncture an organ or use the wrong angle when cutting with the knife," he replied. "I didn't succeed in doing this right away. It took practice. Mostly, you need to get comfortable doing it. If you get dizzy or nauseous, remember you can step away from this for a few minutes."

She bit her lower lip as she turned the knife over in her hands. He'd given her smaller gloves for this task, probably ones he'd worn when he was younger. They looked as if they'd been well used in the past. Of course, the gloves could have belonged to his mother.

"Were these your mother's?" she asked, raising her hands to show him her gloved hands.

"No. My mother wouldn't do this chore."

She wanted to ask him more about it, but she noted the disappointment in his voice and figured she knew enough. His mother hadn't managed well out here. At least, not as well as he would have preferred. Well, that explained why he worried she wouldn't be able to handle it. She was a woman, like his mother had been, and since that was the case, he saw her in the same light he'd seen his mother: weak and delicate.

She clutched the knife in her hand. She could do this. It didn't matter if she was a woman. Why, on the train, she'd heard of a woman who took some acreage and created a homestead. She did this all on her own. And if that woman could do it, then Phoebe could skin an animal.

"You got the string we brought out?" Abe asked her, glancing her way.

Not sure what he wanted to do with the string, she looked at her knife. "Yes."

"You need to tie off its penis."

Her jaw dropped. "I need to do what?" Surely, she hadn't heard right.

"If you don't, urine can get on the meat. If that happens, you'll spoil it."

Oh. That made sense. Even so, this wasn't going to be pleasant. But then, none of this would be. She placed the knife on the clean blanket then picked up the string. The fox was dead. It wouldn't feel anything. She kept telling herself this as she performed the task. When she was done, she hesitated to breathe a sigh of relief. No doubt, this had been only the first of many disgusting things she'd have to do.

"You can use the knife now," Abe said. "You want to cut from the tail," he pointed to it, "and work your way up to the chin." He made a straight line from the tail to the chin. "Don't cut deep, though. Be careful. You don't want to accidently poke the stomach. Also, try not to get any hair in the meat."

That was a lot to do at once.

As if he could read her mind, he said, "Go slow. As long as you don't rush it, you should do fine."

She nodded but took a moment to gather her courage. She could do this. Abe did this all the time. "How old were you when you first did this?" she asked.

"Eight."

"That young?"

"It was just me and my uncle doing this, and my uncle wanted to make sure I could take care of my mother in case anything happened to him."

Surprised, she turned toward him. "Did something happen to him?" What a stupid question. Of course, something did. Why else would Abe be out here by himself when she and her mother got here?

"A white man shot him."

"Was it someone from town?"

"No. He roams around through the mountains. You don't know him." He gestured to the animal. "Your questions won't get you out of skinning it."

"I wasn't trying to get out of this chore," she said, bringing the tip of the knife to the tail. "When did he shoot your uncle?"

He waited until she made the initial cut into the skin before answering. "I was ten."

She looked at him. "Only ten?"

"Cut," he gently reminded her.

As she did, he said, "He wanted a night with my mother."

Gasping, she stopped. "Tell me he didn't get it."

His gaze met hers, and she saw the pain in his eyes. "Would telling you what you want to hear change the fact that it happened?"

"That's terrible," she whispered.

"She had a gun in the house, but she refused to learn how to use it. Knowing how to use a gun makes all the difference. She had time to shoot. She could have prevented it."

"Where was your father when this happened?"

"With his wife, where he should have been to begin with, but I guess if he'd stayed where he belonged, I wouldn't have been born."

She straightened up. It was probably a hard thing to be thankful to be alive, knowing he'd been the product of adultery. Unless... "Did your father do the same thing that man did?" She cleared her throat. "Force himself on her?"

"No. She wanted to be with him." His eyes went skyward. "God only knows what she saw in him. My mother wasn't perfect, but she was my mother."

"And your uncle was alright with it?"

"My uncle didn't like it, but since my father gave him gifts he could use around the place, I guess he made his peace with it, or at least tolerated it."

"What happened after your uncle died? Did your father keep coming around?"

"Yes. Even more than before, and everyone knew about it. Phoebe, I'm never going to live down that shame. I know things are wild out here and that we don't have the same rules they do back East. But even this town can't forgive what happened between them. Do you really want to be the wife of a bastard?"

There he went again, trying to dissuade her from being with him. "Abe, when I look at you, I don't see a bastard. I see a man who works hard and cares enough about me to let me go if I think I'll be happier elsewhere. But I'm not going anywhere. I'm where I want to be."

She turned her attention back to the fox and continued slowly and methodically cutting up to its chin.

ABE WASN'T ALL THAT surprised when Phoebe couldn't eat lunch. He had to skin an animal three times before he was able to eat anything. Unlike her, however, he hadn't felt the need to take a bath. He brought in water from the well while her mother heated up water. He left Phoebe and her mother in the cabin afterwards to give her the privacy she needed. The last thing she needed was him standing around her when she was getting clean, even if they were married.

He decided to tend to the garden so she wouldn't have to. She'd done enough for the day. She didn't need to do any more. When he was done, he went up to the loft and settled back on the blanket. He hadn't gotten much sleep the night before. It was his fault. He should have been more insistent Phoebe go back to the cabin. Otherwise, he wouldn't have held her all through the night with a persistent erection keeping him awake.

He closed his eyes and relaxed. As he did, he couldn't help but remember how pale Phoebe had gotten while she pulled back the fox's fur. She even had to stop everything and walk away for a couple minutes, especially when she had to remove the intestines. But she came right back and continued on. She made a couple of tears into the fur and punctured the heart, but overall, he was impressed she did as well as she did for her first attempt.

This only went to prove that Phoebe wasn't the type of person who made an idle boast. If she said she'd do something, she did it, even if it made her queasy. That was good. It meant she was tough. It meant she could adapt to anything life threw at her. In his entire life, he couldn't think of a single person who'd impressed him more.

"Abe, are you in here?"

He opened his eyes and sat up. Sure enough, Phoebe had come into the barn to look for him. His lips curled up into a smile. He should have known she'd track him down.

"Up here," he told her and waved.

She came over to the ladder and climbed up to the loft. "I did pretty good with that animal, didn't I?" she asked as she sat beside him.

"You did, but don't get a swelled head. As soon as you think you know something, life has a way of reminding you that you really don't."

"Oh, stop being so pessimistic." She nudged him with her shoulder. "Given it was my first time, I was pleased by how well I did. I thought I wouldn't be able to save any of that fox when I started."

"If that's the case, then why were you so careful?"

"I had to try my best. If I didn't, you would have hauled me and Ma off to the stagecoach."

"That's not true." As much as he hated to admit it, he added, "You got the heart of a Cherokee. I should have known it was just a matter of time before you made your point."

She let out an excited gasp and hugged him. "So you'll finally stop trying to get rid of me?"

"Yeah, I suppose," he said, though his tone wasn't as reluctant as he wanted it to be.

"You like having me around," she teased.

Despite himself, he felt his cheeks warm. "Maybe a little."

"You like it a lot." With a playful twinkle in her eye, she added, "I like you, Abe. You're a good man."

"Well, don't let anyone know. It would ruin my image," he joked. "I don't think I could get through the town if people actually approved of me."

She chuckled and reached up to touch his hair. "I like your hair. It's like silk. I wouldn't have thought it possible for a man to have such lovely hair, but yours is one of the prettiest I've ever seen."

Abe grimaced and nudged her hand away. Pretty, indeed! "My hair isn't pretty, nor is it lovely. It's the same hair my ancestors had. They wore it long with pride. I do the same. It separates me from the white man."

"I'm sorry. I won't say it's pretty or lovely. Can I say that of all the hair I've ever seen on men, yours is the best?"

After considering her words, he nodded. Yes, he could allow that.

She ran her fingers through his hair again. When he was young, his mother would comb his hair. He hadn't cared much for it since she also had to work through his tangles, though she'd tried to be careful. The only reason he'd liked it at all was because his mother had been paying attention to him. Not that she hadn't paid attention to him at other times, but this was one of the times when she hadn't seemed to be ashamed of their heritage. She'd made him wear white boy's clothes and only taught him the white man's language. But his hair was one of the few things she'd allowed him to keep.

So he had good memories attached to his hair. Even so, with Phoebe, the experience was different. Her movements were gentle and slow, and in some ways, this made it uniquely sensual. Phoebe wasn't intending for it to be that way, of course. She had no idea what effect she was having on him, especially when she was sitting so close to him, and her breasts were touching his arm.

When he made eye contact with her, he caught sight of something he'd never seen before. Acceptance. There was more than that, though. A deeper look revealed desire and love. The two were so intertwined he couldn't separate one from the other. One thing was clear. She wanted him to kiss her.

His heartbeat picked up as he cupped the side of her face with a shaky hand. The moment seemed suspended in time, and he was aware this was the only chance he had of turning away from where this was leading. There were a million reasons he could think of why it was in her best interest he not proceed with where his thoughts were going, the most notable one was knowing if he did, her future would be tied to his forever. There would be no turning back. She'd be forced to live in a town surrounded by people who would never fully accept her because of her association with him.

She leaned closer to him and closed her eyes, a silent invitation to kiss her. He tried to resist. He told himself she could never really be happy living in a place like this, that he needed to do what was best for her. But the instant her lips touched his, all thoughts of running away departed.

He wrapped his arm around her waist, and he brought her closer to him as he deepened the kiss. She didn't pull away. In fact, she responded very nicely to him, snuggling closer against him and slipped her arms around his neck. The spark of desire their kiss had started was quickly winding its way around him, prompting him to cast aside the last of his resistance.

With a low moan, he traced her lower lip with his tongue, and she parted her lips, allowing him into her mouth. Soon, their tongues were interlacing, and everything around them faded away. All that existed—all that mattered—was the two of them.

He brought his hand to one of her breasts and cupped it in his hand, noticing how soft it was. Up to now, he'd only imagined what it'd be like to touch a woman's breast. It was his favorite part on the female body, though he'd always made sure not to let his gaze linger on there too long, and Phoebe had been no exception.

Since she'd come to live with him, he'd often fought the urge to stare at her breasts, lest he embarrass her, or worse, disgust her. But she wasn't disgusted by the idea of making love to him. If anything, she seemed excited about it, and that only made his erection grow harder.

Still kissing her, he encouraged her to lie back on his blanket then settled beside her. He traced the curve of both breasts over the fabric of her shirtwaist. As wonderful as it felt, his fingers itched to slide under her clothes so he could enjoy her bare flesh.

He'd like to say he was graceful as he unbuttoned her shirtwaist, but the truth of the matter was, those buttons were awfully small, making him struggle through it. Ending their kiss, he gave his full attention to the buttons. She, in turn, unfastened the buttons on his shirt. This mutual exchange of undressing the other was surprisingly arousing and only built up his anticipation for what was to come.

Once he was finished with her buttons, he pulled the chemise up to her neck and took a moment to get his fill of her breasts. They were larger than they looked under the confines of her clothes, something that delighted him to no end. He took his time in touching them. Her skin was soft and smooth, just as he suspected she'd be. The rest of her was the same way, after all. But her nipples were hard. Intrigued, he traced them, noting the difference between them and the white flesh that surrounded them.

"You're so beautiful," he whispered.

Without waiting for her to respond, he lowered his head to take one of the nipples into his mouth. She let out a moan and clasped his arms, her grip indicating her pleasure. Encouraged, he cupped one of her breasts in his hands and continued his ministrations, first paying attention to one nipple then going to the other.

"I'm aching," she murmured at one point while he was tracing the edges of one of her nipples.

Aching? He lifted his head so he could get a look at her. Her eyes were closed, but there seemed to a mixture of pain and pleasure on her face, and he couldn't figure out which one he should go by.

"Am I hurting you?" he asked, hoping it wasn't the case. God help him, but he didn't think he could stop at this point, no matter how hard he might want to.

"No. It feels good. It's just...I think I need you to touch me down here."

She lifted her skirt and wiggled out of her bloomers, baring her legs and the dark blonde patch of curls between them. She spread her legs farther, giving him a generous view of her entrance. His penis strained to get in there, but he wasn't ready for it yet. No. He had so much to explore first, so much to enjoy before he found completion in this act.

She guided his hand between her legs. To his surprise, she was so wet one of his fingers slid in without any effort. She lifted her hips to take him further in, her warmth surrounding him and pulling him in deeper. Unable to resist the temptation, he slid another finger into her, and sure enough, it went in just as easily. He wasn't sure who groaned the loudest, but he couldn't think of anything else that felt this good. Her breasts had felt wonderful, but this seemed even more so.

She lifted her hips again and began rocking them. "Yes," she whispered. "That's what I needed." Then she pressed the palm of his hand against her sensitive nub.

He was so fascinated by her uninhibited motions that he watched her as she rocked faster against his hand. Her expression was still the perfect blend of pleasure and pain, but her moans and raspy breathing assured him she was enjoying everything they were doing. He couldn't recall a time when he'd seen anything more lovely.

Then without warning, she grew still and cried out. Her slick passageway clenched and unclenched around him for several long moments before she let out a contented sigh and relaxed.

She smiled at him. "I didn't think it'd be that good," she murmured then brought him closer to her so he was kissing her.

This kissing, of course, led to him taking off his pants, and before long, he was settling between her legs. She wrapped her legs around his waist and pulled him closer to her so his tip pressed into her entrance. He slid into her until he felt he came to her maidenhead. He pushed past her barrier but grew still when she gasped.

"Phoebe?" he whispered, forcing himself to remain still for her sake.

After a moment, she nodded. "It's alright. Keep going."

He hesitated, but she shifted her hips, which made it easier for him to go all the way into her. There was no way she could possibly know how exquisite this simple action was. He kissed her, letting his tongue brush against hers, and then he proceeded to make love to her. He went slowly at first, just to make sure he wasn't hurting her, and since she brought her hands to his rear end and encouraged him to move faster, he knew she wasn't in any pain. After a while, she was even groaning in pleasure.

He delayed the inevitable for as long as he could, purposely slowing down the momentum of his thrusting and shifting his attention to the trunk nearby. This was the best thing he'd ever experienced, and he had no intention of rushing through it. This was something to be savored. And he found there was greater pleasure to be had in drawing it out. Even she seemed to enjoy it, for she murmured his name and kissed his neck.

When he finally decided to give into the urge to climax, he lowered his head to hers and gave her a long, lingering kiss. Then he buried his face in the nape of her neck and resumed his thrusting. She let out another cry, this one reminiscent of the one she'd let out when she was at her peak. The telltale clenching and unclenching of her core let him know she had, indeed, climaxed again. Groaning, he gave her one more thrust and released his seed. The surge of pleasure coursed over him, coming in waves, one right after the other. Slowly, each wave grew weaker and weaker until he was spent.

He collapsed in her arms and embraced her, thrilled that she still had her legs wrapped around his waist, ensuring their intimate connection hadn't been lost. He'd never felt so close to another person. For the first time in his life, he was whole. All along, a part of him had been missing and he didn't know it until now.

Once he was able to catch his breath, he rose up on his elbows and cupped her face in his hands. Her cheeks were still flushed from their lovemaking, and her eyes sparkled with joy, letting him know she had enjoyed their time together as much as he had.

"I love you, Phoebe," he whispered, caressing her cheeks with the pads of his thumbs.

She smiled. "I love you, too."

He lowered his head and kissed her, not in any hurry to end it.

Chapter Twenty

Two weeks later, Phoebe shot the bottle off the post and turned to Abe with a smile on her face. "I got it. Now you have to give me a kiss."

He arched an eyebrow. "I don't recall us having that agreement."

"I just made it up. For every bottle I shoot, you have to kiss me."

After seeming to consider it, he finally consented and came over to kiss her. She knew he planned on a short one, which was why she put her arms around his neck and drew him closer for a longer kiss. He wasn't hard to convince to linger at her lips. In fact, it was his tongue that brushed along her lower lip, sending a spark of pleasure straight through her. Soon, their tongues were intertwining, and she couldn't be sure, but she thought she heard him let out a low moan.

When their kiss ended, she couldn't resist teasing him. "You don't seem to mind giving me a kiss when I hit a bottle."

Though he offered a shrug, she caught a hint of a smile on his lips. "If it helps you get better at shooting, then who am I to argue? But," he added before she could get another kiss from him, "your mother did say she was going to join us today, didn't she?"

"She did. She insisted on doing the dishes first. I figure we have another five minutes alone."

Despite her suggestive move in pressing her body against his, he said, "If you want another kiss, you have to shoot another bottle."

"You're surprisingly stubborn on these matters, Abe."

"I'm the one who's stubborn? You insisted on staying here with me."

"Which you secretly wanted but was too proud to admit." She nudged him in the side and winked. "It's alright. You can call me your convenient wife if you want."

"Well, it is certainly convenient to have you around." He ran his hands down her back and cupped her behind in his hands.

Figuring he wasn't all that opposed to another kiss after all, she made another attempt to wiggle a kiss out of him, but he shook his head.

"Not until you shoot another bottle," he said. "That was the agreement you made."

She let out a moan but shook her head in amusement. "You're a hard man to please, you know that?"

"If you wanted kisses without shooting a bottle, you should have specified that."

Chuckling, she decided to let him win this particular battle. She stepped away from him and picked the next bottle she wanted to shoot. It took her three tries to knock it off the post, but when she did, she let out another cheer and faced him, waiting for him to give her another kiss.

"I would," he began, gesturing behind her, "but we have company, and I don't think she wants to watch us kiss."

She turned around and saw her mother heading toward them. Glancing at Abe, she said, "You owe me one."

"Don't worry. I'll do more than kiss you later when we're alone," he replied.

The heated look he gave her sent a shiver of pleasure straight through her. Who knew the intimate life of a married couple could be so wonderful?

Abe retrieved the revolver from his holster and gave it to her mother when she reached them. "I'm going to put more bottles up, so hold off on the shooting until I'm back."

"I had no idea he had such a good sense of humor," Phoebe told her mother in a low voice so he wouldn't overhear.

"It's nice to see you in love," her mother replied with a smile. "I was praying you'd find a good man you could be happy with when you started answering those ads."

"Things didn't happen the way either of us expected, but it did work out. It's just as you said. I had to give it time."

"It's easier for someone my age to talk about giving things time. The older you get, the more patient you become."

"Sometimes I'm actually grateful to Carl Richie for doing what he did. I know the way he went about it was wrong, but it brought us here and I've never been happier in all my life."

"That's the important thing. And Abe's just as happy. It all worked out for the best." Her mother's eyes twinkled. "Actually, it worked out better than I hoped."

Abe came over to them. "You sure you feel comfortable handling a gun?" he asked her mother.

"I can handle it," she said. "I just need to brace myself better when I pull the trigger. I won't fall back today."

"At least Abe caught you before you landed on the ground," Phoebe added, unable to avoid laughing. "I warned you there was a kickback."

"Yes, I know," her mother replied, "but you made it look like it was nothing at all to just stand and shoot."

"It got easier the more I practiced," Phoebe admitted. "I don't even think about it anymore."

"Practice makes everything easier," Abe said. "You'll do fine today. Remember to keep your arms and wrists straight out."

As her mother got ready to shoot, Phoebe couldn't help but notice Abe went behind her mother. "You think she's going to fall back again?" she asked him.

"I didn't say that," he replied.

"Don't give him a hard time, Phoebe," her mother said, a sparkle in her eye. "He's watching out for an old woman."

"You have a young heart," he replied.

"Ma does have a young heart," Phoebe agreed. "How old we feel is often in our minds."

"If only the body would cooperate better," her mother mused.

"You do fine for someone your age," Abe said. "It's often how we feel inside that affects what we're able to do. If you believe you can shoot well, you will."

"That's true." Phoebe gestured to the bottle in front of her. "Go for it, Ma. Give that bottle what's coming to it."

Her mother laughed then fired the Colt. The bullet didn't even come close to the bottle, but it didn't go up like the others had. And more than that, she didn't fall back.

"You did better that time," Phoebe assured her. "Try again."

Her mother nodded and shot again. Though she still didn't get close, her aim was even more level with the bottle. "I'm afraid it's going to take me longer than you to get the hang of this," she told Phoebe.

"It doesn't matter how long it takes to reach a goal as long as you get it."

"You're right. When you put it like that, I don't seem so bad."

"You're doing more than some women would do," Abe spoke up. "You'll get there."

Phoebe met Abe's gaze and smiled. She'd underestimated how patient he was. Oh, she knew he was patient. He'd been patient with her while she was learning how to do the chores around the place. But he was especially kind in his instructions, and she couldn't help but love him all the more for it. Yes, Carl Richie had done her a favor by posting the ad on Abe's behalf. She couldn't have ended up with anyone better.

PHOEBE KEPT HER LEGS wrapped around Abe's waist, reluctant to part from him after their lovemaking. The loft was quickly becoming her favorite place. Yes, they usually slept in the cabin at night, but from time to time, they would find a reason to go up into the loft during the day to enjoy each other. More often than not, she was the one who instigated their lovemaking, as had been the case today.

At the moment, he was kissing her neck, his actions now lazy since they'd both exhausted their passion. She sighed in contentment and ran her hands up and down his back. He brought his lips to hers, and soon, their tongues were intertwining.

She was quickly learning there were different kinds of kisses. There were those that they gave each other during the day that didn't lead to more. They were more like a hello or a quick way to say, "I love you." Then there were those that did lead to more. Those had more passion in them. The ones they shared during lovemaking were, by far, the most passionate.

The kiss they were currently sharing was more gentle and slower. It seemed to express a tender thankfulness for the fact that they were together.

When the kiss ended, he asked, "Wasn't I supposed to be teaching you how to ride a horse?"

She offered a playful shrug. "We did make it to the barn."

"Yes, but you cornered me as I was getting the reins, and the next thing I know I'm up here."

She ran her leg down his, noting the way her action made his eyes darken in desire. Besides the kissing, she was quickly learning how to seduce him. "I don't recall you protesting."

"It's hard to protest when a beautiful woman is kissing you and touching you in a certain place."

"That certain place was already hard by the time I touched it." Which was something else she'd learned. When he had an erection, he most definitely wanted to make love. She ran her fingers through his hair and shot him a wicked grin. "You can't tell me you don't feel better when it's inside me. I feel better when it's in me." Then, noting the way he lengthened inside her, she clenched around him.

He let out a low groan. "I'm never going to get any of the chores done if I keep taking you with me."

"But we weren't going to do a chore. We were going to ride horses. Tell me the truth, wasn't it much more fun to do this instead?"

"Alright, yes, it was. This is always going to be more fun," he admitted. "But you need to learn to ride one. What if I get injured or sick and can't make it to town to get the doctor? There are good reasons why you might need to ride a horse. You can't always hook it to a wagon."

"You're right. I might need to ride a horse in the future, and it'd be good to learn how to do it. Everything you're teaching me is useful, Abe. I might get distracted from time to time, but I am a quick learner."

"That's true. You do learn fast."

"See? It'll all work out. Just like with everything else you wanted me to do, I'll learn to ride a horse."

"I want you to learn today."

"I'll learn today. I promise."

She cupped the back of his neck and pulled him down to her so she could kiss him. She intentionally let her lips linger on his. Then, for added measure, she clenched around his erection again, aware he was, most definitely, ready for more lovemaking. Her tongue brushed his bottom lip in silent encouragement for him to forget about the horse for the moment and focus on her.

The ploy worked. He started kissing her in earnest, his tongue sweeping her mouth. Having successfully managed to get him exactly where she wanted him, she opted to urge him to roll onto his back so she could be on top this time.

Then, out of curiosity, she turned her back to him and straddled him, taking him inside her. She leaned forward and lifted her hips. She let him slide partly out of her before she lowered herself back on top of him. She released a groan. She hadn't expected the movement to feel that good, but this particular position was allowing him to stroke a part deep in her core that the other positions hadn't.

Intrigued, she repeated the action, lifting her hips and then bringing them back down. She bit her lower lip and did it a third time. This time, she was rewarded with a moan from Abe. He brought his hands to her hips and squeezed them.

"Don't stop, sweetheart," he whispered then lifted his own hips so he was deeper inside her.

He guided her hips in a rhythm that soon had her rocking over him in earnest, and before long, she reached the peak. Crying out, she stilled, only briefly aware he was still thrusting in her, his movements fast as he sought his own climax, something that served to prolong her own state of bliss. He grew taut, his penis throbbing in her as he filled her with his seed.

After they both descended back to earth, she got off him and snuggled up against him. He brought her into his arms and kissed her, once more showing her how thankful he was they were together. And she, in turn, kissed him back with the same gratitude.

They would linger in the loft for a while and keep kissing, she knew. But then, she'd be good and learn how to ride the horse. It was important to him, and she would do it. Maybe afterward, though, she might talk him into coming back up to the loft for one more tryst before she had to help her mother with supper.

Chapter Twenty-One

Clinking metal scraps broke Abe out of a sound sleep. He bolted up in the bed, taking a moment to process what he needed to do. But only a moment. Those metal scraps served as his only warning. There was trouble, and he didn't have time to delay. His uncle made that mistake, and it cost him his life.

Abe got out of bed and slipped on his clothes, trying to be quiet so he wouldn't alarm Phoebe. It was best she stay out of whatever was going on. No doubt, it had something to do with that day in town when Enoch tried to take advantage of Phoebe. He knew Enoch and Benny wouldn't let the matter go. Those types never did.

Just as he grabbed the Colt from his drawer, Phoebe sat up and yawned. "What's going on?"

"Shh..." He gestured to the open window then hurried over to her. "Someone's out there," he whispered. "I have to take care of it."

Her eyes grew wide, and she suddenly seemed alert. "You think they're here to hurt us?"

"Why else would they be sneaking around in the middle of the night?" Before she could respond, he said, "Go to your mother and hide in the attic in her bedroom. No one will find you there."

He caught the sound of a horse approaching. The person was heading to the barn. Good news. At least for now. It would buy Phoebe and her mother time.

"Get to the attic," he whispered. "I don't want anything to happen to you or your ma."

From there, he slipped out of the room and quietly made his way to the window in the kitchen. In the moonlight that filtered through the trees, he saw someone sliding off his horse. Even in the dark, he could tell who it was because of the man's taller than average height. Benny.

But was he alone? There had only been one round of clinking from the metal scraps. It was possible someone following him managed to bypass the metal. The second person would definitely have an advantage.

Abe went to the window in the main area of the cabin, but he didn't see anyone else. Still, he had to be careful. He lifted his gun and watched as Benny entered the barn.

Was Benny there to give him a warning? If he wanted to hurt him or one of the women, he would have come to the cabin. So by going to the barn, he might be sending Abe a warning.

Sometimes Abe wondered if Phoebe thought he was being paranoid, but at times like this, he thought he wasn't paranoid enough. He probably should have dug holes along the property and covered them up. Then Benny might have fallen into one, and they would all be safe right now. Or he could have laid out a net, which would have caught Benny and captured him. Of course, Benny might have missed the hole or net, but it would have been one more level of protection.

Abe shook his head. No sense in worrying about that right now. If he survived this, he could dig holes or set up a trap to catch someone in a net later. Right now, he had to focus on getting rid of Benny.

He left the cabin, careful to search the property. He detected no one else. Benny was in the barn. Abe decided to take the chance Benny didn't see him and swiftly made his way to the barn. The only thing he had on his side was the element of surprise.

With a glance around him, he saw no one else. Well, so far, so good. He turned his attention back to the barn and peeked in through the opening. Benny's back was to him.

Abe snuck into the barn, glancing once more to make sure there was no one else around.

Benny lit a match and held it above the hay near the trough.

Abe put the gun up to the base of Benny's neck. "Don't drop that," Abe said.

Benny hesitated, holding the match out, and Abe figured the man was weighing the pros and cons of releasing it.

"Who came with you?" Abe asked. Might as well find out who might be lingering in the shadows, waiting to make a move, even if he still didn't see anyone. When Benny didn't answer, he pushed the gun into the base of his neck. "You're on my land, Benny, and on this land there are lots of hiding places. I can shoot you and bury your worthless hide. No one will find you. So if you think I'm not willing to shoot, you got another thing coming."

Assured there was no one in the barn, Abe looked back through the doorway, scanning as much of the cabin as he could make out in the dark.

"Blow out the match," he told Benny.

For a moment, he didn't think Benny was going to do it, but then Benny did.

Abe frowned. That was too easy. Once more, he scanned his surroundings. What else was going on? What was he missing? He grabbed Benny's collar and forced him to arch his back toward him so he could whisper in Benny's ear, "Who did you bring with you?"

"You shoot me, they'll hang you," Benny hissed. "If I go missing, they'll know you did it. I don't care where you hide my body."

Abe gritted his teeth. Benny had set a trap, and like an idiot, he fell right into it. Benny had every intention of Abe finding him, and he was taking a chance Abe wouldn't shoot. But Abe couldn't shoot. Not when he knew doing so would hurt his chances of finding the other person, or people. Benny wasn't the only one in town who'd love to see him hang.

Abe glanced around the barn, wondering where might be a good place for him to hide. As it was, he was too exposed. Anyone could see him. The only thing holding them back from shooting was probably the fact that he had Benny in a delicate position.

Yanking on Benny's collar, he forced him to go with him into the corner of the barn where he could hide in the shadows. He looked around for something to tie Benny up with, but the rope was too far and he doubted Benny would sit still while he retrieved it.

"This is better than you deserve, you piece of filth," Abe whispered before he slammed the butt of the gun on the side of Benny's head.

Benny slumped forward, unconscious. Abe hurried to the window and peaked out the corner of it, making sure no one would see him. After he studied the cabin, he searched for any signs that someone else was there. He tightened his grip on the gun. Someone had to be out there, biding their time to make their move. He just wished he knew who it was and where they were, so he could make a plan to stop them.

His gaze went back to the cabin. He hoped Phoebe and her mother were in the attic. For all he knew, someone could be in there already. It was stupid to leave the cabin. He thought he'd taken care of everything, but he forgot how vulnerable it made a man to have women under his care. If it was just him, there wouldn't be that surge of panic rushing through him right now. This must have been how his uncle felt that night Gene Carter came on their property.

Abe glanced around him, once again making sure no one else was in the barn. No. There wasn't. He released his breath and turned his attention back to the cabin. Maybe there was no one else. Maybe Benny had come out here by himself, wanting to set the barn on fire, to issue a warning. Abe ran his fingers through his hair, pushing it away from his face.

He didn't know what to think. All he knew was that he should have set more traps along the property. Did his uncle go through the same doubts, thinking over all the things he should have done to better secure the place?

What if Abe had overlooked something small but important that would be his undoing? What if he hadn't done enough to protect Phoebe and her mother?

He hated this. He hated feeling helpless. He wiped the sweat from his brow and focused on the cabin while listening to every little sound around him. Was he better off getting to the cabin or staying here? Just what was the exact nature of the threat? He caressed the trigger of the gun. Oh man, if only he knew what to do.

A couple of gunshots fired from the cabin, and he bolted out of the barn. He didn't think to stop and see if anyone was hiding among the trees. At the moment, none of that mattered. All he kept thinking was someone found Phoebe and her mother.

He burst through the front door, holding the gun in front of him and trying to adjust to the darkness inside the main living area. His foot hit someone, and he kicked at the person before thinking it might be Phoebe or her mother. But then, he heard someone shift from behind the couch and aimed his gun toward the sound.

"Who is it?" he ordered, keeping his focus on the couch. All he could see was the shape of a gun and the top of someone's head.

"Phoebe," the person whispered and peered around the edge of the couch. "Is there anyone out there?" She pointed the gun toward the front door.

"Yes, but Benny's unconscious," he whispered in return and took a better look at the person lying at his feet.

It was a man. Enoch? Were he and Benny in this together? He nudged the man with his foot, but the man didn't move. He grabbed the gun from the man and went over to her so he had a good view of the open doorway.

He settled next to her, crouching behind the other side of the couch. "Are you hurt?" he asked, keeping his voice low.

"No, I'm fine," she replied.

He detected a trace of fear in her voice, but he decided not to comment on it. They had more pressing things to worry about at the moment.

"Where's your mother?" he asked.

"In the attic."

Good. As long as she stayed there, he had one less person to worry about. His gaze went to the open doorways of both bedrooms. From what he could see, no one was in any of them, but it was hard to tell for sure.

"Is there anyone else here?" he whispered.

"No. That man came in through our bedroom window, but I was already dressed and in Ma's room by then. I took my gun with me."

Keeping his gaze on the area around them, he asked, "How did you know he came in through the bedroom window if you were with your mother?"

"I had her go to the attic, and I came out to this room." He was ready to criticize her for taking such a risk, but she added, "I could hear him coming in because he tripped on the boots I left under the window in our bedroom. I knew he hadn't had time to see me. I know how to shoot a gun. I might as well do my part to protect our home."

Despite the tense situation, he found himself chuckling under his breath. Yes, she definitely had a fiery spirit in her. "You did good," he finally whispered. "Benny's in the barn. I left him unconscious, but he'll be waking up at any moment. I don't know if there's anyone else. I didn't even know about the one who came in this cabin."

That's what he got for turning his back on the cabin and assuming Benny was alone. He wouldn't make that mistake again.

"I told you I'm here to help you," she whispered. "You take care of one vermin, and I'll take care of another. Then we'll handle whoever else comes."

Well, she managed to get one of them, so he wasn't going to argue with her. He wouldn't have thought it possible when they first met, but she could definitely hold her own. He was both impressed and in awe of her. If he wasn't already married to her, he'd be proposing right about now.

Turning his attention back to the side of the cabin she wasn't watching, he waited for whoever else might pop up. He fully expected it to be Benny. He had only knocked Benny out after all, and given Benny's intense hatred of him, Benny would likely be seeking his revenge.

The minutes ticked by, agonizingly slow as he waited for something to happen. He heard the metal clinking again and held his breath. Either Benny decided to leave or someone else had joined them. Whatever the case, he felt much better knowing Phoebe was with him while her mother was safely out of the way.

When he heard a series of gunshots, he jerked. His first reaction was to see if Phoebe caught anyone, but then he realized the gunfire was outside. He bolted up from the couch, Phoebe close behind.

By the time they made it to the porch, they saw Benny fall to the ground, his smoking gun falling from his hand. Surprised, he looked across the clearing in the moonlight to two men. He couldn't make out the one who was huddled behind a horse, but he could make out Eric who was holding his own smoking gun, still pointed at Benny.

"Don't let your guard down," Abe told Phoebe as he led her over to Eric.

"I knew Benny was coming," Enoch was telling Eric, venturing from behind his horse. "I told you."

"I know, Enoch," Eric replied. "You did a good thing in warning me. You said there are two men, but I only see one."

"I don't know where Gene is," Enoch said.

"Gene?" Abe asked, interrupting them. "Gene Carter?"

"Benny went to Gene," Enoch replied, putting his hat in his hand and squeezing it. "Benny was so mad. I tried telling him it wasn't worth it. He was better off leaving things alone, but he just couldn't. He paid Gene to help him."

"I don't know if Gene's the one in the cabin, but Phoebe might have got him." Abe nodded toward the cabin.

"Before we get too excited," Eric began, "I need to check out the rest of the place to make sure no one else is here."

"We haven't heard or seen anyone else," Abe said then looked at Phoebe to make sure she hadn't.

"No, we haven't," she replied.

"Even so, stay here." Eric took a step toward the cabin then faced Phoebe. "Where's your mother?"

"In a safe place," Phoebe answered.

When she didn't elaborate, Eric settled for a nod and left them.

Abe smiled at Phoebe. She didn't want anyone to know about the attic, which was a smart move in case they ever needed to use it again. "Good with a gun and quick with an answer. You can't beat that combination."

She beamed at his compliment.

Abe's gaze went to Enoch, who was shifting from one foot to another. "You didn't have anything to do with this, did you?"

Enoch shook his head. "No. Benny asked me to, but I said no. I feel awful about what I did to your wife."

Abe wasn't sure if he was telling the truth or not. It was hard to believe whatever white men said, especially those who hadn't shown themselves to be decent in the past. "Yeah, well, if I find out you did, I won't be as forgiving as I was in the general store."

"I think he's telling the truth, Abe," Phoebe spoke up. "He's scared. It took a lot for him to tell Eric what Benny was planning."

"I know it's not enough to make up for what I did," Enoch told Abe. "I don't blame you for not believing me. I wouldn't either if I was you." He lowered his gaze and brushed aside a strand of hair that fell into his eyes. "I am sorry, and I'll never do anything to hurt her or anyone else again. I stopped drinking and am going to live life straight."

Abe wanted to believe Enoch had made a change for the better, but he couldn't. Not until enough time passed for Enoch to prove it.

Deciding the best thing he could do was ignore Enoch, he turned his attention back to Eric. Eric left the cabin and headed for the barn. The three waited in silence for Eric to come out, and when he did, he slipped his gun into the holster. Abe finally let himself relax.

Eric went over to them. "All clear. Abe, I'm sorry. I should have told you I released Benny and Enoch from jail earlier today. My mail-order bride came in, and it wasn't at all like I expected. Anyway, I was planning to come out tomorrow morning to tell you. I didn't think a day would make this much of a difference." He gestured to Benny's dead body and the cabin where the other man lay dead. After a long sigh, he added, "I'll need to take the bodies back to town. Abe, you mind if I borrow your wagon?"

Abe nodded then asked, "Is that really Gene Carter in my cabin?"

"I don't know what Gene Carter looks like," Eric replied. "I only know him by name, and from what I heard, he should be on a Wanted poster."

"I'm going to see if it's him."

Without waiting for Eric to answer, he strode back to the cabin, hoping it really was Gene. Maybe Phoebe and her mother wouldn't be wanting him to be glad someone was dead, but he'd certainly sleep a lot better at night if he knew Gene was no longer alive. Benny was bad enough. Gene was much worse. Gene didn't need a reason to hurt someone. He seemed to make a sport of it.

Once Abe was in the cabin, he lit a kerosene lamp and went to the dead man. He rolled the body over and, sure enough, it was Gene. Phoebe got him in the chest and stomach. With a glance at the couch, he saw Gene had nicked the edge of it. Phoebe was lucky. She almost got it. But since she'd managed to keep a cool head, she won the battle.

No doubt, she could handle anything life out here would throw at her, and that made him feel a lot better about not forcing her onto the stagecoach for her own good.

"Who is it?" Phoebe asked, bringing his attention to the doorway where she stood.

"Gene Carter." Abe wanted to spit on him as he said the name. Since Phoebe was watching him, he forced himself to rise to his feet instead. "He killed my uncle and raped my mother. God only knows how many others he's hurt. You don't need to feel sorry for getting rid of him. You did the world a favor." He walked over to her and hugged her, glad she'd been spared the same fate his mother had to endure. "You keep on getting better with that gun, you promise?"

"Yes, I promise," she told him.

"Good." He glanced back at Gene. "You go on and tell your mother it's safe to come out. I'm glad you didn't tell anyone where she's at. You never know if you'll ever need her to hide there again."

"I told her not to come out unless you or I came to get her."

"Good girl." He kissed her. "Alright, I'll tell Eric to drag Gene's worthless hide to town."

He left the cabin in time to see Eric and Enoch loading Benny's body onto the wagon.

Abe stopped in front of Eric and lowered his voice. "Look, I have a favor to ask of you."

"What is it?"

"As you said, Gene Carter is a bad man. He's done a lot of harm to a lot of people. He killed my uncle, and he hurt my mother. I know the way you white people handle deaths. You give the person a funeral and bury him. It's how you show your respect. I don't like Benny, but he has a brother who's been nice enough to me. I don't mind you giving Benny the funeral and burial out of respect to his brother. But I wonder if you'd deny Gene a funeral and burn his body instead of bury it."

Eric indicated his agreement. "I'll do that, Abe."

"Thank you."

Eric waved to Enoch. "Help me with Gene's body."

Enoch hurried to obey.

Abe followed them to the cabin, his steps slow so they could have time to carry the body out before he reached the porch. When they reached him, he took one last look at Gene's dead body. His mind flashed back to that night he'd shot his uncle and the sneer he'd had on his face while he said, *"Let that be a lesson to you, half-breed. You don't give us what we want, and you'll pay for it."*

Since Phoebe wasn't watching, he stopped Eric and Enoch so he could spit on Gene's face. "I hope you rot in hell."

Taking a deep breath, he indicated he was done, and Eric nodded for Enoch to keep carrying the body to the wagon.

Abe took a moment to regain his composure then went into the cabin. Phoebe and her mother were washing the blood out of the hard-wood floor.

The two looked up at him, and realizing they were waiting for him to say something, probably to reassure them that everything was al-right now, he said, "Eric and Enoch will be taking the bodies to town. They're just about done loading the wagon. We won't have to worry about Benny or Gene anymore." Since he couldn't promise them some-thing like this would never happen again, he added, "I think it's best if we set out more traps along the property. Maybe lay down some nets and dig some holes. Get you," he looked at Phoebe's mother, "shooting better with a gun. You do alright, but you should be as sharp as your daughter."

"We were just talking about that," Phoebe told him. "Ma and I will continue her lessons tomorrow after breakfast."

"We sure will," her mother agreed. "I don't want to be hiding if I can be part of the action."

Abe shouldn't be surprised at the old woman's spunk. Her daughter, after all, had that spark in her. It made sense Phoebe got it from somewhere. But he laughed in surprise all the same.

The women joined him in laughing, and for the moment, the mood lightened considerably, helping to ease the stress from the tense and long night.

Chapter Twenty-Two

A week later, after Phoebe helped Abe set out nets, she helped him dig holes and cover them along key points along the property. As Abe covered the last trap, he said, "That's all I can think of to do to protect us." He turned to her. "None of these may even keep an intruder at bay."

"Abe, you've done all you could. Ma has gotten better at her shooting, and you know I can handle a stranger who comes into our home uninvited. We've all discussed where we'll go and what we'll do next time someone threatens us." She slipped her arms around his waist and looked up at him. "There's nothing worse than sitting back and not doing anything. We've planned out as much as we could, and that makes me feel a lot better."

He drew her closer to him. "I don't want to lose you. You mean everything to me."

She smiled. "You mean everything to me, too. We're in this together."

He returned her smile and kissed her in a way that told her he loved her. Afterwards, he wrapped her in his arms and rested his chin on the top of her head. She closed her eyes and exhaled, hoping he wouldn't continue to blame himself for Gene being able to sneak into the cabin the way he had. The important thing was she heard Gene and was able to hide in a place that allowed her to save herself and her mother from any harm.

Yes, it'd scared her. It would have scared anyone in her position. But she'd known how to shoot a gun, thanks to Abe taking the time to teach her. If he hadn't given her the tools she'd needed to protect herself, who knew if Gene would have found her and her mother? Knowing Gene had been a horrible man was the only comfort she received from killing him.

Abe kissed the top of her head. "I hope we'll never have to go through a night like that again."

"I do, too," she whispered. "But if we do, we'll be ready."

"Yes, we will." After a moment, he added, "As long as we're together, we can do anything."

She grinned. "Yes, we can. And we will. We should get back to the cabin before my mother wonders if we fell into one of the holes you dug."

He chuckled and gave her another kiss. "I suppose we have been out here long enough." Keeping his arm around her shoulders, he led her back to the cabin.

TWO WEEKS LATER, AFTER the judge read the will, he put it on his desk and glanced from Carl to Abe. "I'm sorry, Abe, but Carl has every right to the stream and twenty acres that go with it. That's what your father stated in his will. There's no changing it." He leaned back in his chair and put his hands over his stomach. "Abe, I know you don't like this, but your uncle did sell the stream and twenty acres to your father."

Carl nodded in satisfaction. "I kept telling you I had every right to it," he said, turning to Abe. "Maybe now you'll finally leave me alone."

Abe didn't know what to say. Why would his uncle make that kind of a deal with a white man? After going through the horror of being forced from Georgia and watching his family suffer at the hands of the white men, what force on earth would compel him to sell something as precious? What had his uncle been thinking?

"Things aren't as simple as you're making it out to be," the judge told Carl, drawing Abe's thoughts back to him. "You have to have a legitimate child before you turn thirty. If not, then the stream and land goes back to Abe and any of his children."

"There's nothing in there about a child," Carl argued.

"Yes, there is," the judge replied. "It's toward the bottom of this page." He held up the will and showed it to him. "It's right here if you want to read it."

Carl didn't reach for it right away. He tapped the edge of the chair arm for several seconds, his gaze on the will in front of him. Finally, he reached forward and took it.

This was one time when Abe wished he could read. Even if he'd had a copy of the will, it wouldn't have done him any good. But by the way Carl's face paled, Abe knew the judge had told the truth, that despite the sale his uncle made with their father, there was a chance he could get the land and stream back. And it would be in a way no white man could dispute.

Carl was twenty-eight. He was quickly running out of time. He didn't have to say it. Abe knew desperation when he saw it.

"There has to be some mistake," Carl muttered as he flipped to the first page of the will.

"No, there's no mistake," the judge replied. "I went through the will twice to make sure I understood it correctly. You can see for yourself what I'm saying is true, and that is your father's signature."

Carl scanned the page in front of him and shook his head. "Why would he do this to me?"

"To you? To you!" Abe snapped, straightening in his chair. "You think he did this to you? That was my uncle's land and stream. My uncle was there before your family came along to upset things."

Carl clenched the will. "Your uncle sold it. That's what this document says." He waved it in front of Abe. "You and your mother took everything from me. That land and stream is all I got left. So don't you dare act like this is against you. Right to the very end, you're getting everything. Right to the very end!" Carl bolted to his feet, moving so fast the chair fell to the floor. He shoved his finger in Abe's face. "I hate you! Every day of my life since you were born, I had to live in your shadow. All because our no-good father loved your mother more than mine. And mine was the one who was rightfully wedded to him!"

Abe stood up and glared at him. "Oh, right. Things have been so easy for me. I grew up as a bastard."

"You have so much, and you don't even know it. Why can't you be content with what you already have? Why can't you focus on your wife? Anyone can see how much she loves you."

"I owe it to my wife to give her a stream she can wash clothes in instead of having to pull water from the well all the time."

"That's enough!" the judge barked.

Both men stopped and watched as the judge slowly rose to his feet.

"I understand this is a difficult situation," the judge began, "but the past doesn't change anything. The will is legally binding. Abe, you will not be taking that stream unless it goes to you in the manner the will stipulates. Until then, you two will do no good to argue about it."

"I'm getting that child," Carl told Abe after a long moment of silence passed between them. "That stream and land are the only good things our father left me, and I'm going to do whatever it takes to keep them."

"Carl Richie, what did I say?" the judge asked, turning his cold gaze to him.

With a huff, Carl stormed out of the small courthouse.

Abe took a deep breath to settle his nerves. It wasn't worth it. He could chase Carl down and challenge him to a showdown. The last man standing with the gun still in his hand would get the stream and land. It would be quick and painless. It would finally settle the ongoing dispute. He was better with a gun than Carl.

But he couldn't do it. Not knowing Phoebe and her mother would be disappointed in him. Of all the things Abe could say about Carl, he couldn't say Carl was dumb. Carl knew what he was doing when he posted that mail-order bride ad. He'd selected a young, pretty, and kind woman. He figured all Abe needed was enough time with her, and he'd fall in love and want her to stay with him. Carl knew Phoebe would ultimately be his weakness.

Phoebe wouldn't understand it if he demanded a showdown with Carl. She was from a gentler place where men didn't have a duel over land and streams. Phoebe was a good woman, and more than that, she loved him. She'd been willing to do everything he'd asked of her, but a woman could only be expected to do so much. There was no way Abe was going to risk losing the one good thing in his life.

Forcing back the frustrated tears that sprang up in his eyes, Abe told the judge good-bye and slowly made his way out of the building, squinting at the bright sunlight that bore down on him. He supposed a hat was practical, but there was no way he'd ever wear one.

He was half Cherokee and proud of it. Someday, he might even have children, and he'd tell them the stories his uncle had passed on to him. More importantly, he was going to tell them they should never be ashamed of their heritage. No one was going to make them think less of themselves. He'd have to give up the land and stream, but he wasn't going to give up instilling the right values to his children. And really, that was more important anyway.

Releasing his breath, he turned and headed for Lois' house where Phoebe and her mother waited for him. On this day, however, he didn't look away from other people when they stared. This time, he decided to meet their gazes head on, and to his surprise, a couple of the men offered a friendly nod. He hadn't seen that before. It took him a moment to return the greeting, realizing it was the polite thing to do.

And he couldn't be sure, but he thought the women didn't edge so far away from him as he passed by. But maybe it was all in his mind. Or maybe, just maybe, there had been the few people who had always been willing to give him a chance, but he hadn't noticed it until now. It was hard to tell for sure.

He was just two blocks shy of Lois' house when Carl's wife called out to him. Surprised since she rarely made it a habit of talking to him, he stopped and looked over his shoulder. She was following him down the dusty road. He couldn't be sure, but he thought she'd been drinking by the slight wobble in her steps.

When she reached him, she said, "I just found out about the will." She covered her mouth and giggled.

"I don't see what's so funny about it," he said, wondering where Carl was. Certainly, he'd brought her to town, and Abe couldn't imagine he'd want her talking to him. "Shouldn't you be with your husband?"

"That's what's so funny," she whispered. "Carl's determined we'll have a child together, but between you and me, he'll never get into my bed. So you have nothing to worry about. That property you two have been fighting over since your pa died will be yours in two short years."

Letting out another chuckle, she wished him a good day and went back toward the heart of town.

Abe didn't know where she was going, nor did he care. She was Carl's problem. As he continued his walk to Lois', the reality of it all sunk in. She was Carl's problem. He'd seen the way she and Carl argued, but it hadn't occurred to him just how miserable Carl must be until that moment.

Unlike Phoebe, Carl's wife wasn't easy to fall in love with. She was probably downright impossible. Imagine a wife intentionally sabotaging her husband's chances of inheriting something his father left him. Phoebe wouldn't do that. The fact that it was important to him would have compelled her to do everything possible to help him.

He wasn't used to feeling sympathy when it came to Carl Richie, but in this one instance, he couldn't help but feel sorry for him. Carl had to live with her every day. There was no escaping it.

Having Phoebe in his life made Abe aware of how important a good wife was in a man's life. And, that being the case, his life was actually much better than he'd realized.

His heart lighter, he finished the path to Lois' house and knocked on the door.

Phoebe opened it, and, with concern in her eyes, she stepped onto the porch and shut the door. "What did the judge say?"

"He said Carl has the rights to the property," he told her. "My uncle sold it to my father, and if Carl has a child in the next two years, he gets to keep it."

"I'm sorry, Abe. I know that's not what you were hoping for."

He glanced back at the town and saw an unhappy Carl helping his equally unhappy wife get into the wagon. Turning back to Phoebe, he said, "You know, I had time to think, and in all honesty, it's alright. I have you, and that's more than I'll ever need." He cupped her face in his hands and smiled. "I'm the luckiest man in the world."

Then, without waiting for her to reply, he lowered his head and kissed her, looking forward to their future and the children they would one day have.

Don't miss out!

Visit the website below and you can sign up to receive emails whenever Ruth Ann Nordin publishes a new book. There's no charge and no obligation.

https://books2read.com/r/B-A-MDLI-RMIHC

BOOKS 2 READ

Connecting independent readers to independent writers.

Did you love *The Convenient Mail Order Bride*? Then you should read *Eye of the Beholder* by Ruth Ann Nordin!

Mary Peters despairs that she will never marry. At nineteen, she has no prospects of finding a husband, so she takes matters into her own hands and becomes a mail-order bride. When she arrives to Omaha, Nebraska to meet the man she's due to marry, he takes one look at her homely appearance and rejects her. But fate has other plans for Mary. Dave Larson happens to be nearby and thinks she will make a good wife. Though she is stunned that someone as handsome and as kind as Dave would ask her to marry him, she accepts. She knows that this marriage will not bear the fruits of love. Love, after all, is for beautiful women. Isn't it?

Read more at https://ruthannnordinauthorblog.com/.

Also by Ruth Ann Nordin

Chance at Love Series
The Convenient Mail Order Bride
The Mistaken Mail Order Bride

Husbands for the Larson Sisters Series
Nelly's Mail Order Husband
Perfectly Matched
Suitable for Marriage
Daisy's Prince Charming

Marriage by Arrangement Series
His Wicked Lady
Her Devilish Marquess
The Earl's Wallflower Bride

Marriage by Bargain Series
The Viscount's Runaway Bride
The Rake's Vow

Taming the Viscountess
If It Takes a Scandal

Marriage by Deceit Series
The Earl's Secret Bargain
Love Lessons With the Duke
Ruined by the Earl
The Earl's Stolen Bride

Marriage by Design Series
Breaking the Rules
Nobody's Fool

Marriage by Fairytale Series
The Marriage Contract
One Enchanted Evening
The Wedding Pact
Fairest of Them All
The Duke's Secluded Bride

Marriage by Fate Series
The Reclusive Earl
Married In Haste
Make Believe Bride
The Perfect Duke
Kidnapping the Viscount

Marriage by Necessity Series
A Perilous Marriage
The Cursed Earl

Marriage by Obligation Series
Secret Admirer

Marriage by Scandal Series
The Earl's Inconvenient Wife

Misled Mail Order Brides Series
The Bride Price
The Rejected Groom
The Perfect Wife
The Imperfect Husband

Nebraska Prairie Series
Interview for a Wife

Nebraska Series
Her Heart's Desire
A Bride for Tom
A Husband for Margaret

Eye of the Beholder
The Wrong Husband
Shotgun Groom
To Have and To Hold
His Redeeming Bride
Forever Yours
Isaac's Decision

Pioneer Series
Wagon Trail Bride
The Marriage Agreement
Groom for Hire
Forced Into Marriage

Wyoming Series
The Outlaw's Bride
The Rancher's Bride
The Fugitive's Bride
The Loner's Bride

Standalone
A Deceptive Wager
An Earl In Time
Her Counterfeit Husband

Watch for more at https://ruthannnordinauthorblog.com/.

About the Author

Ruth Ann Nordin has written over 100 books, most of them being Regencies and historical western romances. As fun as writing is, she has also learned that time with family and friends is just as important. She has also learned that writing for passion is the best reason to write since it is what sustains an author's work for the long haul. That's why she's been able to keep writing for as long as she had. It's hard to believe she started out in ebooks back in 2009. How time flies.

Read more at https://ruthannnordinauthorblog.com/.

Ingram Content Group UK Ltd.
Milton Keynes UK
UKHW020702050623
422889UK00017B/2166